PC

POLECAT BRENNAN

A Commander Shaw Novel

Philip McCutchan

Hodder & Stoughton
SYDNEY LONDON AUCKLAND

Copyright © Philip McCutchan 1994

First published in 1994 by Hodder and Stoughton
A division of Hodder Headline PLC

The right of Philip McCutchan to be identified as the Author of
the Work has been asserted by him in accordance with the
Copyright, Designs and Patents Act 1988.

10 9 8 7 6 5 4 3 2 1

All characters in this publication are fictitious
and any resemblance to real persons, living or dead,
is purely coincidental.

British Library Cataloguing in Publication Data

McCutchan, Philip
Polecat Brennan
I. Title
823.914 [F]

ISBN 0 340 60025 X

Typeset by Avon Dataset Ltd, Bidford-on-Avon

Printed and bound in Great Britain by
Mackays of Chatham PLC, Chatham, Kent

Hodder and Stoughton Ltd
A Division of Hodder Headline PLC
47 Bedford Square
London WC1B 3DP

POLECAT BRENNAN

So Polecat Brennan was alive. This was according to Max. There was, I suppose, no reason why he shouldn't be alive. He'd been released from prison around eight years ago; he'd be no more than fifty now. But once I'd seen him dead – or thought I had. Later, it had turned out that the mangled body lying in the road, a jammy mess below a high-rise council block in London's East End, had been a neatly planted lookalike.

Polecat Brennan, a very vicious killer, apprehended and gaoled, had lived on.

According to Max again, Polecat had a lady friend. Her name was Steenie Ogmanfiller and she was an American. Ogmanfiller was an unusual enough name. I remembered Edie and Chester Ogmanfiller. I remembered them in Spain, tourists from Lewiston, Idaho. They'd got mixed up in some very dirty business centred around a sect called the Flood Fearers, weirdos who'd built themselves an ark because they believed the world was about to be inundated once again. Inundation or not, both the Ogmanfillers had come to a very gruesome watery end in a flooded cave system. Even now, years later, I could see Edie Ogmanfiller's bloated breasts, big enough even in life, when both the dead Ogmanfillers had sped past me on the flood in torch-lit gloom, somewhere beneath Andalusia and the mighty Sierra Nevada.

The Ogmanfillers, and likewise Polecat Brennan, had also been involved with two outfits that were basically opposed to each other: CORPSE, which letters stood for Committee of Responsible Persons for Selective Eradication. And WUSSWIPP, which stood for World Union of Socialist Scientific Workers for International Progress in Peace.

CORPSE had been extreme right wing; WUSSWIPP had of course been Moscow-based. Old hat now. The old order had gone for good, thanks to Gorbachev and Yeltsin. Communism was a dead letter, as dead as I wished Polecat Brennan was but wasn't.

And Max had confirmed a relationship: Steenie Ogmanfiller, aged twenty-seven, was the Ogmanfillers' granddaughter.

So what was in the air? Back in the Flood Fearer days, Polecat Brennan, basically a WUSSWIPP man, had infiltrated the CORPSE organization – out for his own ends, of course. CORPSE had had megalomaniac plans that had almost come off – plans to station big tankers laden with nuclear explosives off all the major British ports in order to put pressure on the Brits (and I'm summarizing this very briefly) to surrender all power to a Rightist backlash to be supported by a large number of Establishment figures inside the country who were squirming under the then Labour Government.

All in the past. But the key to the future, as they say, often lies in the past. So what did the juxtaposition of Polecat Brennan and an Ogmanfiller descendant portend?

Max hadn't had a clue. But he'd been worried about CORPSE, the Rightist group. If they were still extant: in fact, they'd not been heard of for years. Most of the big boys had died when I'd arranged the blowing up of the monster Japanese tanker off the Bloody Foreland in County Donegal. But Max had made one point.

He'd said, 'Germany. United Germany.'

'Is there a German connection?'

Max shrugged, spread his hands palms upwards. 'I don't know, Shaw. It's worth bearing in mind, though. There's a very sizeable Nazi resurgence in Germany. You know that.'

I did know it. Anti-Jewish sentiments, the desecration of Jewish burial places, the rise of the little Hitlers and the Görings, the Himmlers and the Goebbelses, the petty strutting would-be Gauleiters, the reappearance of the swastikas, the awful shadowy threat of the reconstitution of the concentration camps, and now – for what it was worth but everything, however whacky, had to be taken into account when Polecat Brennan was believed to be involved (in what?) – now there was the new concept of a joint German-French military corps, an armed force that would exclude Britain and NATO. It didn't take much grey matter to arrive at the conclusion that that corps would turn out in the end to be backboned and led by Germany rather than France.

3

* * *

When I had got the word on my car radio that Max
wanted to see me immediately – and with Max
'immediately' meant five minutes ago – I'd been
driving south along the M1 with Felicity Mandrake,
with Scotland and a skiing holiday behind us. I hadn't
expected the call of duty quite so soon. The summons
was clearly urgent. I said, 'You'd better come with me.'
We were accustomed to working together.

'Max hasn't asked for me.'

'Never mind that,' I said.

I filled up with petrol at the Scratchwood service area
and then drove straight to the City and Max's penthouse
suite in 6D2 HQ. Max was the head of the British end of
6D2, which was a worldwide organization – these days
it even extended beyond what had been the Iron
Curtain, leaving out only China – for gathering
intelligence and then going right in and where necessary
bowling out the villains. We were unofficial and yet at
the same time official in so far as we worked largely for
governments and when we did, then the sky was the
limit as to what we could get away with just so long as
nothing rubbed off on the shining image of the
government concerned. Or governments, in the plural:
there was a lot of international co-operation.

I glanced at my wristwatch as I drove into the
underground parking lot of Focal House a little after
16.30 hours. The lift took us up the fourteen floors of
HQ to Max's suite and we ran the gauntlet of Max's
personal secretary, Mrs Dodge.

Not much of a gauntlet today: 'He's waiting,' she said crisply. She used the intercom. We were bidden in. Max, Big Max as he was known to the outfit, was standing at one of his shatter-proof windows looking out over his helicopter landing pad, or what could be seen of it through the rooftop garden's winter tracery. 'Big Max' was apt; he had the build of a world heavyweight champion.

He swung round. Max didn't waste time on idle chatter or enquiries about holidays. And that was when he told me.

'Polecat Brennan,' he said. 'Familiar, Shaw?'

'Very,' I said at once. 'Southern Spain – '

'I have the details. He's surfaced again.'

I waited. Max always spoke when he wanted to and not before. This time he said abruptly, 'Sit down, both of you.'

We sat. Max went to his enormous tulip-wood desk and lit a cigar. He offered the box to me. I said I would prefer a cigarette and he produced a box of specially made cigarettes that he always got from the Burlington Arcade, from a firm that had made them initially back in the 1930s to the order of the then Prince of Wales. The aroma was better than any cigar.

Max blew a cloud of smoke. He said, 'Frankly, I'm puzzled. I don't know much but I suspect plenty. I suspect plenty just because Polecat Brennan's involved. He's lain low since he came out of gaol some years ago. I have to admit we'd lost track of him. He did a very good job of disappearing. Not that he's actually appeared – not to me. But I had a message. By telephone.'

'Brennan himself?'

'Not Brennan. An old contact of yours – he'd tried to get you rather than me, but you were gallivanting about the Cairngorms. Cello Charlie.'

I knew Cello Charlie all right. Cello because he'd once played the cello in a works orchestra when he worked as a machine minder in a factory producing electrical goods. He was an OAP by this time and a nasty little rat and once he'd been on the outer fringe of WUSSWIPP, just a peasant in the organization but very left inclined. WUSSWIPP had finally done the dirty on him and ever since he'd hated their guts. And he was a useful nose, always provided you kept it clean for him.

'So what did Charlie say?' I asked.

'Little enough. He sounded scared, as though enforced death was close behind him. Because I wasn't you, he was very cagey. But he did say that Polecat Brennan had been in London and was keeping some unusual company.'

'How unusual?'

'For Brennan – very unusual. A French cabinet minister, he said. A supporter of Le Pen. He wouldn't give me the name on the phone.'

Le Pen, I thought, staring at Max. The leader of the extreme Right in France, a leader with large and increasing support from the voters.

I asked if there was any more detail.

'Not a thing,' Max said. 'No name. Charlie cut the

call and that was that. The point is, he wants to meet you.'

'And?'

'And,' Max said with a cold smile, 'I suggest you go. Ten thirty tonight. At the Neutered Cat — Soho.' That was when he told me about Brennan's lady friend, Steenie Ogmanfiller, granddaughter of the flood-drowned Ogmanfillers of yore. And then he'd spoken of reunified Germany.

I told Felicity to take the BMW back to the flat in South Kensington alone. I had some research to do in the Focal House computerized filing section, the micro-films. Before I met Cello Charlie — I'd be back when I could. Don't wait supper, I said. She told me to watch it; I told her the same thing. We'd been together a long while now. Max didn't like emotional involvements of his agents but that had been one row he didn't win. Take it or leave it, we'd both said, and he'd taken it. But we were always worried about each other's safety and I understood Max's point well enough.

I went down a number of floors to the files and I recalled Polecat Brennan from computerized oblivion. It was just an exercise in memory refreshment: I hadn't carried all Brennan's details in my mind all those years. Too many other assignments had intervened.

He came up on the screen, nastiness in vivid green light.

Of course, he hadn't been christened Polecat. Richard de Valera Brennan had been born of Irish parents in Plaistow, London, on 25 December 1944, a real Christmas baby in the middle of World War Two. He'd been one of seven sons and four daughters. His father had been a labourer, aged forty-five at Polecat's birth, and he'd been in the ARP as one of a heavy rescue squad. Not long after the birth of what was to be the last child, he'd been scattered by one of Hitler's V2 rockets. The mother had subsequently had a series of liaisons and eventually Polecat, a tearaway even at three years of age, had been taken into care as being beyond her control.

There was a list of misdemeanours: setting fire to bedding, bashing up other youngsters, acquiring a knife by means unknown and using it on Matron, who had nearly died as a result. That sort of thing. Leaving the institution at the age of sixteen, he'd got a job as a laundry-van driver's mate, hefting laundry boxes. He'd got the sack and a spell in borstal after attempting to rape a young housemaid in the basement of a house in Eaton Square. That was the real start of his criminal career: on emergence from borstal he fell in with a gang of hoodlums living on their wits. A number of prison sentences had followed: GBH, robbery with violence, more rape. There were a number of killings that the police had never quite managed to pin onto him until at last they got him when, being drunk at the time, he drove a car at a crowd of children waiting at a bus stop, killing three of them and severely injuring two more. Polecat Brennan, never once expressing any remorse, went down for manslaughter: the prosecution never managed to prove intent and the alternative charge was the one that stuck.

Coming out, Brennan had been recruited by WUSSWIPP, then a very potent organization, for employment in the lower echelons. In short, as a strong-arm minder.

From then on, I needed no refresher course. The events in Spain and all the other places that assignment had led me to were still vivid.

I put Polecat Brennan back to bed in the computer and took a long walk through to Soho. I had plenty of time in hand. I had a leisurely drink and a meal at Ley On's.

Then I drifted around and took a preliminary look at the outside of the Neutered Cat. It was a nightclub and a very sleazy one, with a paint-peeled door in which was a spyhole. Behind this door would be a sort of gorilla, the sort that passed you in and chucked you out if you got nosey. As ever, I was comforted by the Biretta in my shoulder holster.

'Well, Charlie.'

'Long time no see.'

'Let's cut the clichés, Charlie. What's in the wind?'

I'd passed the door gorilla, who was in drag. I'd mentioned Cello Charlie, which was good enough. I'd found Charlie perched on a stool at the bar, not drinking but chatting to the bartender who happened to be a quite nice-looking girl. I bought drinks, paying with two twenty-pound notes and getting little change.

Of course, I had a virtually unlimited expense account but I hoped the session was going to be worth the money. Even 6D2 keeps an eye on overdone expenditure.

Charlie led me to a quiet corner; as quiet as was possible considering the monotonous drumbeat coming from half a dozen speaker points.

He answered my question. 'Polecat Brennan,' he said, casting anxious looks around.

'That's right,' I said. 'So?'

'He's in London.'

'You're sure, Charlie?'

' 'Course I'm sure. See him I did.'

Charlie looked indignant; his professional competence had been doubted. He was a little weasel of a man with a big head in both meanings of the term, and as shifty as a stoat, but with me he'd always been reliable. And he'd certainly know Polecat Brennan: he'd been done up by him once.

'I apologize,' I said. 'Where and when?'

'Going into Ashley Gardens. Dunno which flat.'

Ashley Gardens was a big block not far from Victoria Station, more or less behind the Army & Navy Stores.

'Right,' I said. 'When?'

'Evening before last. Just after eight thirty.'

'You didn't follow him up, then?'

Charlie gave a long-suffering sigh. 'Lift, isn't there? Short of going — '

'All right,' I said. 'Point taken. You weren't going to stick your neck out.' I supposed prudence was a virtue, and certainly Charlie was pretty far removed from the typical Ashley Gardens resident; he'd fade better into the background of a dosshouse.

'Go on,' I said.

'Bloke with him there was.'

'What bloke?'

Charlie fidgeted a little. He'd heard the keen interest in my voice and he'd always had an eye to the main chance. 'Goin' to cost you,' he muttered, his glance flickering over my face.

'You know I'm generous. Let's have it.'

'Well – okay, then.' He paused, picked at his nose. Charlie was a compulsive nose-picker and it tended to put one off one's drink. The thought of eating in his company was shattering. 'Frog bloke,' he said.

That much, I'd had from Max. 'You don't happen to know which Frog bloke?' I asked without much hope.

'I do know, see.' There was an air of triumph. 'Gaston dee Saint Aycreev.'

I nodded. Gaston de St Ecrive was not in fact the cabinet minister Charlie had postulated via Max; but I knew he was a high official, a civil servant in the French Foreign Ministry. Certainly he and Polecat Brennan made interesting bedfellows. I wondered who the tenant of Ashley Gardens might be: presumably not the French bloke, and Polecat Brennan struck me as equally unlikely. But, of course, you never knew and Brennan could, almost certainly would, have a new identity.

I asked, 'How do you know the French bloke was M de St Ecrive? Come to that, how do you know he was

French?' Even if the man had spoken, I doubted if Charlie would recognize a French accent from a Greek one or any other. And, on the phone to Max, he'd mentioned Le Pen. For Charlie, that was erudition run wild.

Charlie picked his nose again. 'Sewer Rat,' he said.

'Oh, yes?'

'Know him, do you?'

'Who?'

'Who I said. Sewer Rat. No, you don't, do you? That's what they call him — never did know 'is real name. Works in the sewers 'e does. Brighton,' he added.

'So?' I couldn't really visualize any connection.

''E's one of those. You know what I mean?'

I said I thought I did. 'You'd better explain in full,' I said.

Charlie leaned closer. While he was getting his thoughts together I saw that his glass was empty. Charlie, I guessed, was well known to the Neutered Cat and probably, for services rendered — for instance, being a two-way nose, tipping them the wink about any police interest — got his drinks free or anyway at cost price. I let his glass stay empty; they wouldn't be giving *me* any rebates.

Charlie said, 'This bloke, Sewer Rat — he's a customer here when 'e's in London. Young bloke, good-looking — gets pissed easy. Heard him talking, see. With this Froggy. Frog seems to come over to Brighton quite a lot.'

'Is he,' I asked, 'one of those too?'

'I reckon so, yes. Well, I heard the name Brennan spoke and then I remembered you'd had an interest like, years ago.'

'You've a good memory,' I said.

Charlie grinned. 'Need to an' all in my line. Anyway, I reckoned you'd like to know more, right?'

'So you followed them?'

'Followed the Frog bloke.'

'And Sewer Rat?'

Charlie shook his head. 'No. The two o' them, they went upstairs like, you know how it is. Just the Frog come down, or anyway come down first like . . .'

'And left?'

'Right. So I followed him, like I said, after getting 'is name from the bar girl. He went into the Regent Palace, in the bar. Met Polecat Brennan. Brennan didn't recognize me, but I recognized 'im all right.'

Again I said, 'Good memory.'

'I'd cause to remember 'im, didn't I? Mind, 'e'd aged. Looked even nastier.'

'He would. Good work, Charlie.' I paused. 'Anything else?'

Charlie shook his head. 'Just they walked across the park after and I tailed like. Didn't risk getting close enough to hear any talk.'

I said, 'Ears to the ground, Charlie, keep me informed.'

Then I said, 'This Frenchman. When you rang Max, you said he was a supporter of a man, another Frenchman, a Monsieur Le Pen. How come, Charlie?'

'They talked about him in 'ere, that's all. Seemed important to the Frog, don't know about the Rat.'

The Frog and the Rat — it sounded like *The Wind in the Willows*. In the past Polecat Brennan had meant extreme danger and I didn't like the political implications of his being apparently involved with the extreme Right in France. And Max had spoken of Germany. Currently there was nothing more to be got from Charlie, so I left the club after slipping some tens under the table into Charlie's hand. In Piccadilly I flagged a taxi and sat back in a fair amount of deep thought. Gaston de St Ecrive came across often from France to meet the boyfriend — weird boyfriend, working in the sewers, but that didn't have to signify. All sorts of people did all sorts of jobs these days and we had John Major's assurance that we were now a classless society. But I didn't believe for a moment that the Frenchman came across to Britain solely for the boyfriend. That would be just something on the side, a mix of business with pleasure. When I'd known him, Polecat Brennan had certainly been no gay and I didn't see him in that context at all, a threesome. The Polecat, the Frog and the Rat.

Oh, no.

The Brennan connection was the principal aim of Gaston de St Ecrive.

Two days later I read in the papers that St Ecrive had committed suicide. No reason given or prognosticated. Maybe his proclivities had been about to face exposure. Or maybe it was something else.

* * *

I didn't take the taxi all the way to the flat, stopping the driver a couple of turnings short. Inbuilt security: agents of 6D2 lived and breathed circumspection. Max was hot on one hundred per cent security: you never led tails home, and you always assumed a tail.

I checked for the tail as the taxi drove away: that was second nature.

Nothing.

I walked on home. I was hungry and it was probably too late to go out for a meal now. But Felicity was a very good cook so I wasn't bothered.

Not then. Not as I walked towards the flat.

Not until I heard the scream, a desperate sound of pain and blind terror coming from ahead. I saw the light in an open window of the flat − Felicity was a fresh-air fiend even in winter − and I saw it go out as I broke into a fast run. There was no reason why the scream should have come from the flat but I had a hunch. I pounded up the steps and into the lobby. No signs of trouble. I used the lift. I put my key in the lock of our door: it hadn't been tampered with. I called Felicity's name and there was no answer. I searched the flat. It was empty. I went to the fire escape, out onto the platform below the window at the end of the passage. The window was still open and as I went through my shoe slipped on something sticky.

Blood.

I went down the fire escape like greased lightning. There was no sign of Felicity but heads were coming out

15

of windows. As I reached ground level in the parking lot behind the flats, I heard a car start up in the street beyond, a very powerful engine by the sound of it.

I ran through but the car had gone. Sod Max, I thought viciously. If I hadn't obeyed his instincts that had become mine, if I'd taken that taxi right to the door – I might just have been in time.

2

There was no point in getting the BMW out and mounting a road chase. I went back up the fire escape, two steps at a time.

I was about to pick up my security line – the telephones appeared to be intact, anyway at first glance – and alert the duty officer at Focal House when my outside line burred.

I grabbed the handset.

'Commander Shaw,' a voice said – not asked, said. I waited. The voice, a man's and one I didn't recognize, went on: 'We have Mandrake.'

Hoarsely I said, 'So?'

'Because of that, you will have care in what you do from now on out. You understand?'

I asked a silly question. 'Who is this calling?'

There was a soft laugh. 'We shall be in touch,' the voice said. That was all: the call was cut. No demands mentioned, but of course there had to be some. The fact of those demands to come meant one good thing: in the meantime, Felicity wouldn't be harmed - not lethally at any rate.

I thought fast. Max had to be informed, of course.

They, whoever 'they' might be, would expect that and it wouldn't rub off on Felicity. Or anyway I had to hope so.

I took up the security line and spoke to Focal House. I said, 'At this stage, it's for information only.' I didn't want too much action for now and neither would Max be likely to sanction it. To mount a search would be pretty useless, real needle-in-a-haystack stuff that would get nowhere. In cases like this, you just waited for the other side to make the first move. Waited as patiently as you could, biting your fingernails to the quick.

Polecat Brennan?

I couldn't say from the voice. From my memories of him, I couldn't be sure. But I didn't think it was Brennan. Brennan would be in the background, not sticking his neck out so early in the game.

I prowled the flat, looking for clues, anything that might help. I didn't move anything. The Focal House fingerprint section would be going over the place shortly but I didn't really expect them to find anything helpful. Polecat Brennan, if he was behind this and for my money he had to be, was no amateur, no fool. And at first sight no traces of anything had been left. No sign of a struggle, nothing misplaced. Just the open window giving onto the fire escape and the blood that would be Felicity's.

That apart, it was just as though she'd gone out — like taking the dog for its night walk, if we'd had a dog. Her scent was in the air, everything in the bedroom was intact, reminding me of her. The bed was ready. I had a moment of blind hatred for Polecat Brennan. If he'd shown then, I'd have torn him into bloody shreds.

The phone burred again: the security line.

Max in person.

'Get round here right away,' he said. He didn't sound too friendly.

It was no particular surprise to find that Max was still at Focal House; he often worked late and not infrequently he slept overnight in the penthouse suite where everything was always laid on – kitchen, bathroom, staff of one manservant always in residence, the lot.

First came the bollocking as expected. 'You're a bloody fool,' Max grated, his eyes seemed to bore right through me. Then he had the grace to add, 'And so am I, for permitting it.' He was referring to our relationship, Felicity and me. 'It's what I always feared – you, laying yourself and the organization open to threats of this sort. And it's not the first time it's happened. However, it's done and I'll say no more for now.' He looked away from me, lit one of his cigars and shoved the silver box of cigarettes across his desk towards me. I took one. 'Have you any ideas?' he asked.

I said, 'Polecat Brennan.'

He nodded. 'Anything else?'

'No.' I told him about the scream, the open window, the blood on the fire escape's platform, the sound of the car pulling away fast, the subsequent telephone call.

He said, 'Softly softly.'

I raised my eyebrows.

19

'That's the way we play it,' he said.

'Agreed.' Wait, in other words, as I'd already known would be his response.

He said abruptly, 'It's not coincidental that I'm still here, Shaw. And I don't know how much coincidence there might be around in other directions − the fact is I was summoned to the FO just as I was about to go home. They're asking for our co-operation.' He paused. 'The Foreign Secretary himself. What I'm about to tell you is top secret. Understand?'

'Understood,' I said.

'Pierre Monet − French Foreign Minister − he's due to visit London on Friday week, which of itself is not secret, of course. At the same time *our* Foreign Secretary's visiting Paris.' He looked up from his desk. 'Did you know about this?'

I said no, I didn't.

'On the face of it, it's curious. But there's a reason. It's a kind of − of goodwill thing is the nearest I can get to it. It's linked in with TML − Transmanche Link. A symbolic exchange of ministers, French and British − bullshit really, more cement for the EC and all that blah.'

'So what's the secret?' I asked.

'This: French security has dug up a threat to Pierre Monet. Put briefly, he won't reach England alive.'

'Who's behind it − and why? What do they want?'

'It's not known who's behind it but to forestall your next question, it's not believed to be the French Far Right. The Foreign Secretary suspects a German connection, the neo-Nazis. As to what they want — again we don't know. It's going to be up to us in 6D2 to find out. Our Bonn agency's been alerted, of course. Likewise Paris. And I want you to liaise.' He paused and then said what I was expecting him to say. 'Miss Mandrake's disappearance — there could be a connection. Agree?'

'It's possible,' I said. Then I asked, 'How is Pierre Monet travelling — by air?'

Max shook his head. 'No. I mentioned TML. He's coming through the tunnel. At the same time, the Foreign Secretary's going through the other way.'

That led me to another question. 'Is there any parallel threat to Humphrey Chatterton?' Chatterton was the British Foreign Secretary.

'No,' Max said. 'Why do you ask?'

I said, 'The tunnel. You said — at the same time. Is that the fact?'

Max nodded. 'The idea is, they cross on the way. Symbolism again.'

Well, of course the tunnel hadn't been open all that long and the wondrous concept had been a sort of British-French love affair right from the start. I said, 'Food for thought, isn't it?'

'You mean an attempt in the tunnel? It's been taken into account, naturally, but not very seriously. Damn it, man, the security in and around the tunnel is two hundred per cent plus! In any case, there's plenty of much easier ways of bumping off Monet than a tunnel assassination.'

* * *

Max sent me down to the political section four floors below the penthouse, and after a session with John Forbes who ran the section and had been dragged out of bed earlier by Max, I went home. There had been no further visitations so far as I could see and I went to bed though not to sleep for thinking about Felicity and that highly expensive and ultrasecurified Channel tunnel. I knew, and even more so should Max, that there is no such thing as total security. The terrorists can always find a way. The IRA bombing campaigns in the heart of London over the years had been ample proof of that. The bandsmen in Hyde Park, Victoria Station, Staples Corner, Bishopsgate, the van close to Downing Street − there were too many for complete recall.

This time, it evidently wasn't the IRA. I thought about the political implications. If the French Foreign Minister should be assassinated by Max's hypothetical German Right - what then for Europe? What would be the likely consequences?

John Forbes had been dour about that. The EC had been somewhat rocky ever since the Danes had rejected the Maastricht Treaty back in 1992. That rejection had shaken Jacques Delors badly, though it had delighted plenty of people in Britain on both sides of the political fence. I had often thought that no one, not even France and Germany, really wholeheartedly wanted to have any truck with the EC, the whole concept of a Federal Europe.

France and Germany . . .

The whole thing revolved around them.

And now? Or rather soon — if the threat developed?

Real trouble, and that maybe was exactly what lay behind it. The break-up of the EC. If so — and really that was a pretty long shot since plenty of patching up of relationships would be put swiftly into gear — but if so, then I would be quite prepared to accept the assassination equably. But I had to stifle such thoughts: my job was to assist in ensuring the safety of Pierre Monet and not to have political opinions in the course of duty. However, I was British. I still thought of myself as a British citizen, not a European one. So, I was dead certain, did Max.

Ashley Gardens?

Cello Charlie had seen Brennan going into Ashley Gardens with what he'd called a Frog. A recce around that part of Westminster?

No. Keep that for later — hold onto the knowledge obtained from Charlie until it could be made more effective use of. Brennan, just in case, wouldn't be around Ashley Gardens at this particular time.

Wait — that was all I could do. It wouldn't be long before contact was made. Thinking of Felicity, I did at last drift off into an uneasy, nightmare-ridden sleep until, at eight fifteen by the clock on my bedside radio, the phone burred. Not the outside line.

Max.

'FO,' he said. 'You've an appointment at 10.00 hours. A man named Hedge, in Security. I wish you

23

luck – he's next in line to the assistant under-secretary. And knows it.'

The call was cut. I got out of bed, bathed, shaved, had breakfast – cornflakes, toast and marmalade, coffee, two cigarettes. Whilst shaving I'd seen how haggard I looked. I had a very deep love for Felicity Mandrake.

This man Hedge, behind a tight security barrier of officers seconded from Scotland Yard, plain-clothes men under a detective chief superintendent, a man called Simon Shard whom I'd once met on an earlier 6D2 assignment, inhabited a very opulent office only a little less luxurious than Max's penthouse suite at Focal House. He sat behind a big desk, rising somewhat perfunctorily as I was shown in by his confidential secretary. On the desk I noticed a packet of Rennies: indigestion sufferers could be hell on wheels. I recalled that Shard had said his boss was just that and more. Thick was the word he'd used.

Hedge, two pisspots high and fat and pompous, said, 'Ah. Yes. Commander Shaw. I've spoken to your chief, of course.' Having uttered this self-evident fact, he paused. 'I – er – I understand the 'commander' is a naval rank, not a police one?'

'Right,' I said. 'Much retired now, of course . . .'

'Of course. But it's such a relief, don't you know.'

I didn't know quite what to say to that, so I just said, 'I'm glad of that, Mr Hedge.'

'You've no idea,' he said, and waved an arm towards a chair. 'Do sit down.'

'Thank you.' I sat. He went on, 'The police. Well. Oh, they have their uses, I'd never deny that. But they have police minds, don't you know. Rigid.'

I felt tempted to say, like civil servants, even those in the God Almighty Foreign Office. But of course I didn't; it seemed as though I was probably going to have to work with this Hedge and I would have to make the best of it.

He placed a Rennie in his mouth and sucked a little. He became brisker. 'This threat,' he said. 'Nasty. We're very worried.'

'Yes,' I said into what had become a longish pause: briskness had wilted a little. 'So am I.'

'Quite. I – er – understand you have a personal involvement in the shape of – of a – er – young woman.'

Shape. It was a good word in connection with Felicity. She had a wonderful shape. But I didn't like the way Hedge had spoken; there was a kind of disparagement in his words and voice, as though Felicity was just a tart. I said rather sharply, 'A fellow agent of my organization has been kidnapped. My personal feelings . . .'

'Oh, quite. Quite. I understand fully.' He was glossing over what he might be seeing as a gaffe. 'Duty's duty and – er – well. The point is this, Commander: do you yourself see a connection with the threat?'

I said evenly, 'I don't know yet. Early days. I'm waiting for a contact.'

'That's all?'

'Not quite,' I answered. 'It may be coincidence, but I don't believe it is.' I paused. 'I take it we're speaking in complete confidence, Mr Hedge?'

He laughed. 'My dear fellow, this is the Foreign Office!'

I said, 'Yes, it is. But I'd like an answer, please. Yes or no. Just the two of us, because my further knowledge has so far been between myself and the London chief of 6D2.' I saw no need to mention Cello Charlie: Hedge might have had a fit if he knew about the initial gleaning of secrets from a down-and-out.

Hedge said very stiffly, 'Oh, all right. *Yes.*'

So I told him all I knew about Polecat Brennan. And – again without naming any sources - about the Frog. And about Sewer Rat. His face was a study. The Foreign Office wasn't used to such things. But he took the point that if Polecat Brennan – and by inference Felicity's disappearance – was involved with a homosexual French senior civil servant who supported Jean-Marie le Pen, then things might indeed be very, very nasty.

I stressed, however, that so far we had nothing actually on Brennan. The past was the past. And Brennan *might* not be involved in Felicity's kidnap.

'Yes,' he said. 'I follow. I trust you'll keep me informed of developments.'

I pointed out that I took my instructions from Max. He nodded at that and went on to say that my services had been requested for undercover FO liaison only. The Foreign Secretary and the Prime Minister both wanted this thing kept so far as possible under wraps, did not wish for any overt governmental involvement at all, preferring it to be handled exclusively by 6D2 until perhaps official action should become inevitable.

I knew, or any way guessed, the reason for this and I came out with it flat.

'Because if things to wrong — if there's any cockup and the assassination takes place — it's 6D2 that'll carry the can?'

He gave me a dirty look: they didn't talk about cockups in the Foreign Office. He said, very stiff again, 'You may place any interpretation upon it you wish, Commander.' I think he was now seeing me as just another sort of rough, common policeman. He waffled a bit after that, saying it was undesirable for the British Government to be seen to involve itself in matters between extreme political parties on the Continent (and never mind the EC, I thought). Governments dealt not with terrorists but with other governments . . . on and on, load after load of bullshit that meant nothing whatsoever except that Whitehall was going to keep its nose clean for as long as possible.

He didn't impart any useful information.

Why?

Because he hadn't got any.

And neither had I, really. Just supposition about Polecat Brennan.

That interview was a waste of time. Except that I had made a point of sorts: that I was still Max's man first and foremost and I wasn't going to compromise 6D2 if I could help it. Before we parted Hedge asked me what I proposed to do.

'I don't know yet,' I said, and that was the honest truth. A large part of sleuthing consists of waiting for something to turn up, some information to come to hand. You are not everlastingly chasing around in fast cars or crashing into insalubrious dives like, say, the Neutered Cat and arresting everyone in sight. As Max had said: softly softly.

And softly softly is a strain on the nerves. The more so when there's the personal angle. I'd raised the question of the Channel tunnel with Hedge; he'd been as dismissive as Max. The security, Hedge said, was absolutely watertight and who would be so foolish as to attempt anything where they were certain to be bowled out before they could move a finger?

Or plant a bomb, I'd suggested. The look he gave me was intended to put me in my place: political assassins these days don't go about their business with little round bombs with smouldering fuse lines attached. Cloak, dagger and black mustachios, that look had seemed to say, were out. Of course, he had a point. We're all very sophisticated now. But Semtex, for instance, doesn't carry a lighted fuse and it can be very easily concealed and it doesn't react to customs or security probes. On the other hand, I did know, of course, that it was always a nightmare to the security people and the TML authority that one day some lunatic might try something and as a result the security really was good. I'd seen some of it for myself: a year or so previously I'd been down to Folkestone to look around the Eurotunnel Exhibition Centre alongside the rail tracks leading into the tunnel.

It had been very impressive, ultrasophistication. I'd seen the mock-up of the control system, the continual monitoring by television cameras of the whole undersea setup, from both Folkestone and Calais. Every one of the six hundred trains that would traverse the tunnel each day had full fire-fighting parties aboard. No chances were being taken; I'd gone into the security angle. Any trouble would be isolated by sealed and fire-proofed doors aboard each shuttle. Outside attack − as a one-time naval officer my thoughts went straight towards depth charges − would quite simply be not on. The tunnels were at a minimum depth of 80 feet below the sea, in some places 150 feet, and they were set in a chalk marl layer that was entirely impermeable to water, while an extra waterproof seal was provided by the concrete lining of the tunnels themselves. Above the chalk marl layer was hard grey chalk, and beneath the tunnel it was gault clay, also water-impermeable. It was all a lot tougher than the pressure hull of a submarine.

I remembered that visit to Folkestone for another reason: I'd had Felicity with me. We'd had coffee at the exhibition centre and then we'd driven on to Hythe for a trip on the miniature railway that ran to Dungeness and the power station. Waiting for the train we'd sat on the grassy bank of the old Royal Military canal, built nearly two centuries earlier to carry supplies to the coastal forts standing against Napoleon − and how Napoleon would

laugh if he could see Britain now, held at the whim of
La France.

Politics again, and that amorphous threat.

But that day there had been no threat, no dangers. It
had been a lovely day in all respects.

Where was Felicity now?

3

The phone rang shortly after I'd got back to the flat; when I wasn't sent elsewhere by Max, I was keeping close to home, expecting the call.

Sweating, I answered.

'Yes?'

'Commander Shaw?'

This time it was a woman's voice, a young woman's voice I believed. I said, 'Yes.'

'Please listen carefully. Miss Mandrake is well.' I detected an American accent, faint but unmistakable. The voice continued. 'It's entirely up to you if she remains well. I guess you understand. Right?'

'Right,' I said somewhat thickly. 'Just tell me what it is you want.'

There was a light laugh. 'I guess you're not that naive, Commander. Nor are we. Your telephone – it'll have a tap on it.'

It had. 'We prefer to talk to you in private. You'll be picked up outside your flat – two minutes from now. Just make sure you call off any tail. You don't, you know who suffers. You got that?'

'I got that,' I said, and added on the off chance, 'Steenie Ogmanfiller.'

It had been a long shot but the intake of breath told me it had found its target. 'Give my regards,' I added harshly 'to Polecat Brennan.' I cut the call then. No point in hanging on: the tap would already have picked up the caller, who would in any case be moving on fast now, well away from some anonymous callbox.

Two minutes. I took up my security telephone and called Focal House. I spoke to the duty officer. 'Report pronto to Max,' I said, 'contact made. A pick-up outside my flat in about one minute.' There was one of our agents on surveillance outside, very anonymously, and I knew he would report my departure. There wouldn't be time for a tail to get there: Steenie Ogmanfiller or whoever wouldn't be lingering once I was aboard. Just the same, I made the point plain. 'No tails, I say again, no tails.'

The lion's mouth was opening. I knew that. But there was no other course. From now on out I had to use my wits, and use them fast. I had the Biretta in my shoulder holster, but of course they would have that off me double quick. I knew that too. I knew something else: Max, when he got the report, would go mad. But I was thinking of Felicity. Maybe I was a bum agent after all, and Max was dead right about personal relationships. Not that it would have made any difference: you don't just fall out of love by order of the boss. But after this was over, I was going to insist that Felicity retired. We might even get married.

32

I went down, out into the street. I didn't see the man on obbo but I did see the Jag drawn up at the pavement and I saw the two men, plus the driver, inside. No Polecat Brennan. The rear nearside door was pushed open and one of the men beckoned.

I got in, clambered past the nearer of the men to sit in between the two of them, where a gap had been left. They didn't speak; they didn't look as though they had the intelligence. They were simple thugs, Brennan's strong-arm boys. They were as alike as two brothers, which maybe they were: pig eyes, negligible foreheads, bulging muscles − and I was right about the Biretta. It was off me almost before I'd sat down.

The Jag pulled away, smooth and fast. When it got to the end of the road a black bag was pulled suddenly over my head and then an arm reached from either side and forced me down so that I was squeezed into a bundle, invisible from outside, on the floorboards.

It was a longish drive through London's traffic, then a speeded-up journey as we came clear of congestion − onto a motorway, I guessed − and then more slow driving. I grew very stiff, being bent in half. When we stopped it took me a while to unwind and while I was unwinding I heard a rattling sort of sound which I took, correctly as it turned out, to be a garage door being pulled down behind. When I was able to get out I was led through another door into the passage of a house, a well-carpeted passage that led to a room with the curtains drawn across the windows. I was able to see all this because on emerging from the Jag the black bag had been removed, and I'd also seen that the Jag's side windows had curtains across them as an extra precaution in slow-moving traffic lanes.

And now I saw a woman, a girl aged at a guess around twenty-five who could be Steenie Ogmanfiller.

I asked her if this was the case. She said yes, and how was it I'd known that?

I said, 'I knew your grandparents. In Spain, years ago. Before and after death.'

'After?'

'After.' I said. 'They swirled past me on some fast-moving floodwater. Underground. It was nasty.'

She shrugged. 'Maybe it was at that. Me, I scarcely knew them.'

'Neither did I, after death,' I said.

'There's no need to be crude.'

'I feel crude. Where's Miss Mandrake?'

She didn't answer that. She said, 'You haven't answered my question. How did you know my name when I called you?'

'I get to hear things,' I said. 'I hope you're happy with Polecat Brennan.' Steenie Ogmanfiller was no beauty: flat sort of face, flat chest, long dank hair, mouse-coloured, and she had bad acne. There was also an unwashed smell about her; perhaps she and Polecat Brennan were the only ones who'd ever looked at each other closely; of course I didn't know what the setup between them was. It could have been strictly business. Very likely it was.

One of the car thugs who'd come in behind me and were in fact clutching my arms asked, 'Want 'im duffed up, do you? Make 'im talk?'

'Not yet,' she said.

I asked again where Felicity was.

'Not here,' she said. 'Somewhere safe. For now. As I told you on the phone, it's up to you whether she stays safe. I don't suppose I need to tell you some nasty things can happen.'

'So what do you want?' I asked.

She said, 'Assistance in the right place.'

'What exactly is that supposed to mean? You want information?'

'Not quite that,' she said. 'Not quite that.'

It was really quite simple, at any rate from the Ogmanfiller point of view. What she and her bosses wanted was a fifth column: me, handed back safe and sound for duty with 6D2. I was to act as the spy inside the camp, following instructions as passed from time to time. Information would come into it as well, of course. But basically I was to manipulate affairs in 6D2 so that the assassination path would be eased. She didn't tell me anything about her organization's plans as such, but she did tell me what Max had already told me as reported from French security: Pierre Monet was to die. And I was to assist in bringing about his death.

If I didn't?

One guess only: Felicity Mandrake.

I was in a very cleft stick. Max was going to love this. If I told him. But if I did that, the end result would rub off on Felicity.

I gave Steenie Ogmanfiller the only possible answer: Get stuffed.

'Okay,' she said. 'You asked for it.'

She gave a sign to the thugs behind me. I was frogmarched out of the room, through a door opposite the one I'd been brought in. Along another passage and then through another door that opened into pitch darkness. A musty, dank smell, not unlike an Ogmanfiller smell, came up. One of the thugs operated a switch on the wall outside and electric light came on below a flight of stone steps.

A cellar.

'Down you go, mate,' the thug said. He urged me forward sharply, and let go of my arm. I fell down the steps, headlong, collecting a few potential bruises. I sat up at the bottom. The door above was banged shut and then the light went out, but not before I'd seen a television screen in one corner, heavily protected by a mesh of metal bars.

Now what?

In the total darkness I got to my feet and carried out as much of a recce as was possible. It didn't help much. I felt around the walls: the brick felt damp from the outside earth and in one corner there was a slop of water that smelled foul when disturbed by my foot. I could perhaps be near water of a sort – sea, river, marsh, water meadows. But not necessarily: the filthy smell could indicate proximity to a leaking cesspit for all I knew.

Just one thing was sure: there was positively no way out. And come to think of it, another certainty: I was to be softened up.

And I believed the softening up would concern that television set.

How right I was.

Obviously operated by remote control, the screen, after a while flickered greenly into brilliant light, the more brilliant because of the otherwise total darkness. Not BBC, not ITV, no happy adverts for banks or building societies, Brekko or ever-so-soft toilet paper, nothing like that.

Closed-circuit TV and just Felicity, plus two masked men.

Felicity was stark naked. She looked utterly terrified and her wrists were tied above her to a wooden beam that ran across just below the ceiling of the room she was in, which looked as bare as my cellar. One of the masked men held a whip. That man was a little, thickset, short runt and although I couldn't see his features I believed it was Polecat Brennan.

The whip went into action. I saw Felicity's body give a sort of jump, and I heard her scream.

I turned away. But I heard more screams. Then there was a voice. This time, unlike the one on that first telephone call after Felicity had been taken, I recognized as that of Polecat Brennan, recognized it for certain.

Brennan said, addressing me as though he were able

to see me face to face, 'You're her only hope, Commander Shaw. I believe you will understand now.'

What could I do?

What would be any man's reaction?

Just a word from me, a word of agreement uttered to Steenie Ogmanfiller, that flat-chested, acne-ridden monstress – she would have to be a monstress to connive at what was happening – what would happen in the end – to Felicity. My word would stop all that. Or so it had been said.

It was not in me to let Felicity suffer.

It was also not in me to be a fifth columnist. I didn't give a kick in the crutch for Pierre Monet, but I didn't see myself as acting against my own country's interests, if such were involved and according to the FO man, Hedge, if only by inference, they were; nor did I see myself letting Max down.

Well, that was for the future. There had to be a way out somewhere. I would find that way. For the present there was only one response for me and when, some while after the TV screen had gone blank and the light had come on and the door at the top of the steps was opened, and Ogmanfiller stood there with the thugs, and said that if I refused to play I would stay there and watch the TV, I gave it.

'You win,' I said.

I was released, once again by Jag and black hood and the rest. Before we left, I was given a lecture, or pep

talk. All about how the slightest lapse in my
'assistance', or any tiny hint that I might have opened
my mouth unwisely, and retribution would be exacted
on Felicity. I might from time to time receive reminders
– not, of course, by television. Maybe a fingertip, that
sort of thing, through the mail. That was if I needed to
be kept in line. For what it was worth – and I had no
alternative but to accord it value – I had Ogmanfiller's
word that her and Brennan's part of the bargain would
be kept: once Pierre Monet was dead and the Brennan-
Ogmanfiller setup was clear and away, then Felicity
would be released.

They didn't say where; and they wouldn't say why
Pierre Monet's death was so essential. They just didn't
say anything beyond the stark fact of the threat to
Felicity, whose eventual (and nasty) death would be
directly attributable to me. They did drop hints about
various forms of nasty death: deep water with heavy
weights attached, incarceration in hard-core used for
motorway construction, dismemberment and acid
baths, things like that. I asked Ogmanfiller if she didn't
think they were still taking a rather large risk.

She just smiled at that. I took her unspoken point: no
risk at all. I hadn't learned anything I hadn't already
known before and I didn't know the location of the
house I was leaving. Only that it was, or might be, near
the sea, or a river, or some water meadows, or a spring,
or a leaking cesspit.

Not much help.

* * *

I wasn't released in London. I suppose I might have been somewhat conspicuous, being bundled out of the back of a car, bent in two like a hairpin. After a longer drive than before – most of it, I think, motorway – the Jag stopped and the black bag was removed and I was pushed out. I was in a side road, a country road with no white line down the middle, not even a B road. As soon as I was out, the Jag moved off fast. Of course, I had its registration number, for what that would be worth: it would have to be a false number-plate, but I would check.

I started walking along a road fringed with winter-sleeping rhododendrons. After a while a Range Rover came up from behind. I thumbed it; the driver was a young woman, very county-looking – I could imagine the green wellies – and all she did was give me an up-yours sign, very ladylike. I didn't blame her: I expect I looked somewhat ragged and it's foolish to take risks.

I walked on. And on: the road that had no turning. God alone knew where I was; but at long last I found a road sign, pointing one way to some place called Handcross and the other way to Turner's Hill. I carried on ahead, to Turner's Hill. Before I got there I came to a larger road with traffic, and I thumbed a lorry, which stopped. It appeared I was in West Sussex and the lorry was going to Brighton, so, since there would be a train there, I went to Brighton too. I'd been left with all my possessions including my notecase with credit cards and cash, so that was okay. (They'd also restored my Biretta, which was a kindly act.)

On the train journey to Victoria I had time, now that the immediate problem was solved, to think ahead about what I was going to do in regard to Max.

There were only the two alternatives: either I made a clean breast or I kept quiet. If I went for Alternative A I would risk Felicity. If I went for Alternative B . . . I didn't like it one bit, the prospect of living a lie, a kind of double life. I would probably come unstuck with dire results to all concerned. But I remembered the words of Ogmanfiller: immediate retribution on Felicity if they had the slightest doubt about my good faith.

Maybe there was a middle way. Keep quiet for as long as possible, see the way things went. Softly softly in other words, if not quite in the way that Max had meant it.

Tricky: but it could be the best way. When the time came to confess to Max, my name would stink; but that was in my view the lesser risk.

The train slowed into Victoria Station and I hadn't made up my mind. I walked through the barrier to the concourse. This was winter, January, and there were not so many American tourists around, so I was able to get a taxi without too much waiting. As ever, I stopped the taxi short of my road and walked through to my flat — our flat, though only with me in it now. I wondered for how long. The French Foreign Minister was due in London, Max had said, on Friday week. Today was Thursday: eight days to lift off. In the interval anything could happen.

I identified our man on watch: he was smoking a

cigarette in the lee of a hoarding where some building work was in progress. I let myself in and went up to the flat. I'd been there for little more than a couple of minutes when the phone burred, the outside line. I answered.

'Yes?'

'Commander Shaw.' It was the Ogmanfiller voice. 'Don't forget.' That was all; and I wouldn't forget. She cut the call. I guessed she'd probably rung several times while I was on my journey back. I imagined her acne flaming with impatience and no doubt a degree of anxiety as to what I might be up to. As it happened, her warning was timely from her point of view. I had hardly put the handset down when the security line cut into my thoughts.

Max.

'Where the devil have you been, Shaw?'

I said, 'Here and there. Trying to get a lead. Without success, I might add.'

That committed me, at least to what I'd thought of as the middle way.

There was a grunt from Max. 'That bloody man Hedge wants you,' he said.

4

The bloody man Hedge, Max said, wouldn't come to Focal House and didn't want me to go to the Foreign Office again. Nor would he use the phone, not even the security line between the FO and Focal House. He'd sent a written message by a minion from FO security.

I asked, 'Where do I meet him?'

'Piccadilly Underground station.'

'Which is a biggish place – '

'I know that. Just walk round and round. You meet as though by sheerest chance. When Hedge has finished with you I want to see you.'

He cut the call. I left the flat, feeling in need of a meal, but Hedge would be awaiting me in half an hour's time precisely. I took the tube, got out at Piccadilly and ascended the escalator to somewhere beneath Eros. I walked round; my watch said that Hedge was late, but soon after that I spotted him, round and fat and wearing (as he'd been wearing when I'd met him at the Foreign Office) a black coat, short, with dark pinstripe trousers. This time he was wearing a bowler and carried an umbrella and a neatly flattened newspaper. I approached, but took care not to look as though the meeting was in any way expected. Hedge, when he acknowledged me in a very cloak-and-dagger way, smiled matily and made some remark about the weather.

I said, 'Yes, isn't it?'

'Seasonal, of course. Mustn't grumble. I'm so glad to see you, my dear chap.' He laid a hand on my arm. 'Going my way, are you?'

I said I was.

'Good show, good show.'

He already had the tickets, which I thought was a little stupid. If anybody *had* been tailing either of us . . . but I didn't say anything. We went down into the depths and caught a tube to God knew where and (I hoped) back again. The compartment was pretty full but we found two seats together and Hedge unfolded *The Times* and held it in front of his plump strawberry-coloured face, speaking thereafter from the side of his mouth and now and again casting keen glances round the paper's other flank. I didn't think he need have worried. There was a schoolgirl next to him on the one side, me on the other, and next to me was a middle-aged lady wearing the uniform and gold stripes of a WRNS officer. Her bray when she spoke to her companion gave me the distinct impression she was no phoney. The legs lurching against us from the aisle belonged to four hippies or ravers or whatever, all of them swigging from cans of lager and one of them playing a guitar.

Hedge was quite safe to speak, and speak he did. What I gathered, none too easily, was that his security boys had dug up a positive connection between Polecat Brennan and a French Fascist extremist.

'Le Pen?' I asked, very sotto voce into *The Times*. Hedge didn't like the use of the name. 'Oh, for heaven's sake, kindly be *discreet*! Not — the name you mentioned. No. That person is entirely in the clear. *Entirely*. A — a man of repute — even if his views don't always find favour with the Establishment. No, I refer to . . .' The voice sank even lower, then rose high. '*Do* you mind? You've just stood on my toe.'

He'd been addressing the nearest hippie or whatever; luckily the hippie was polite. 'Sorry, squire. Jus' keep your fuckin' feet from under and they won't get trod on, okay?'

Hedge seethed. 'Such people,' he hissed at me. 'Scarcely civilized.' Then he resumed, being more careful with his fuckin' feet. 'Louis X,' he whispered.

'Ah.'

'You know of him?'

'Not under that name. Is it a name?'

'It's all that's known namewise. Also a German. Gerhardt von Defflinger-Zwickau.'

'I don't know him either.' The tube stopped at a station and the WRNS officer disembarked, waving a hand back at her erstwhile companion. Her place was taken by the hippie with the guitar; he continued playing. Hedge said sideways, 'Both rabid anti-EC. You get it?'

'Not entirely,' I said.

Hedge clicked his tongue. 'It begins to come together,

does it not? These people are out to sink the EC, more or less as has been prognosticated I rather fancy.'

'How do they sink it?'

'Well, by assassinating you know who – probably on British soil. And then attribute the blame to a *British* assassin, which in fact it seems likely it will be.' He paused. 'Our friend – with the curious nickname, who'll be spirited away safely afterwards. If you're with me.'

'I'm with you,' I said. 'I just don't really see how the dastardly act is going to bring about the collapse of the EC, that's all.' Hedge was the sort of person who somehow brought out words like dastardly. There followed a lot of waffling around what was probably the point, if only I could make it out. Frankly, I couldn't, not really. One way and another Hedge said, there was a lot of ill-feeling in the Community, which was far from the happy union it was supposed to be. Notwithstanding patient work by Britain after the hoo-ha over Maastricht, each country seemed to be at every other country's throat. It wasn't surprising, to me at any rate; no nation likes being told to restrict its fishing, inhibit its farming and alter its road-building programme in accordance with the dictates of some bureaucrat in Brussels. I muttered something like this and Hedge gave me a bad-tempered potted history lesson: the United States had had its teething problems more than a hundred years ago and in the end the individual states had dropped their narrow outlooks and had come happily together to form the most powerful group of states in the world. But only, I pointed out, after they'd fought an extremely bloody civil war.

Hedge said angrily, 'Let us stick to the point, shall we?'

'Gladly,' I said. 'If we can first establish what the point is.'

'I find that offensive.'

'I apologize,' I said. The train rattled on. I seemed to have put Hedge off his stroke.

He said no more until we had reached Turnpike Lane, where he muttered, 'Next stop.'

'H'm?'

'Wood Green. I leave you there.' The train started again; the schoolgirl had disembarked, her place being taken by a man in Securicor uniform. That, no doubt, seemed safe enough for further speech. Hedge said, 'A lack of trust, don't you know. Widespread throughout the Community. An assassination – well, it wouldn't help. The French, you know, so touchy. I put it down to a sort of national inferiority complex. The war and all that.'

We reached Wood Green and Hedge got out. So did the hippies; I hoped he'd watch his fuckin' feet. Hedge didn't say what he was going to do in Wood Green, which didn't seem to me to be much of a centre of EC affairs, or assassinations – he could be on private business. Maybe he kept a mistress in Wood Green, nicely anonymous to Foreign Office eyes – though really he didn't quite look the part.

I caught a train back to Piccadilly. I pondered on

47

French inferiority complexes due to the war and all that. The war was a very long time ago. Nearly fifty years since it had ended. True, the French hadn't come out of it in a blaze of glory: Vichy, the collaborators, the stupid Maginot Line that the Germans had outflanked as soon as it was convenient, the way the French Army had collapsed in 1940. But they'd made up for it later: General de Gaulle, and the many heroes of the Resistance.

Hedge was a fairly typical British civil servant of bygone days. He'd looked to me to be verging on retirement.

I obeyed orders as received in my flat before the Hedge rendezvous: I reported to Max in Focal House. On the way I reflected that Max, on the phone, had made no specific reference to my report as made that morning to the duty officer, about the pick-up outside my flat. He could scarcely have forgotten. Even if he had, he was going to click by the time I reached the suite. But I'd already worked out something to cover that. Or, anyway, I had to hope it would cover it.

It was the first thing Max asked about. 'That contact. What happened?'

'A blank,' I said.

'How's that?'

'Rotten luck on their part. Car had a slight accident.'

'Inspired by you, Shaw?'

I shook my head. 'No. Hit a traffic island — driving too fast. Driver hadn't got his seat belt on — got knocked out. In the confusion I managed to scarper.'

'Where was this?'

I plucked a district out of the air. 'Elmer's End,' I said.

Max made a hissing noise. 'Why did you back out? I would have assumed you'd have followed up, having started. So why didn't you?'

Awkward question, but foreseen. I said, 'I didn't want to involve the outfit.' 6D2 was known internally as the outfit. 'If the police came along. You see, a crowd had gathered and I believe the villains saw it the same way as I did.'

'They didn't try to stop you?'

'Not noticeably, no. They'll find it easy enough to make another contact, so why should they worry? So far as they're concerned, nothing's lost.' I added, 'Of course, I got the Jag's registration.'

Max snorted. 'Fake plates, obviously.'

'Fake plates,' I agreed. 'I checked it through with Swansea. Not exactly fake plates,' I added. 'They'd belonged to a Fiesta reported scrapped.'

Max was swallowing it; I could sense that. He had other matters to talk about anyway. He wanted to know about my meeting with Hedge.

I said it had been pretty abortive but at least he'd given me a couple of names. I trotted them out: 'Louis X,' I said, 'actual name unknown. And Gerhardt von Defflinger-Zwickau.'

'Anything known about them − to the Foreign Office?'

49

'Just that Hedge's security boys have dug up a connection with Polecat Brennan. And that they're both violently anti-EC. Do we know of them?'

Max said, 'As before this moment, I've never heard of them. I'll be checking. Nothing else?'

I shrugged. 'A load of waffle.' I added that Hedge expected that an assassination by (as he'd seemed to infer) Polecat Brennan was likely to wreck the Community. Max didn't pooh-pooh that as I'd thought he would. He said it wasn't entirely unlikely, the way things were, but he also said that our job in 6D2 was, principally, to preserve the life of the French Foreign Minister. The rest was politics, and we were not politicians.

'Nor civil servants.' I said.

'Precisely,' Max said, and I knew just what he meant. Our methods were not always orthodox. I had *carte blanche* — just so long as I used discretion.

Max said, 'Keep me informed, Shaw. Let me know immediately there's another contact.'

Not once had he mentioned Felicity Mandrake. Not even in connection with the Jag. That I took as a kind of rebuke.

I had not, in fact, contacted Swansea. I hadn't had the time what with one thing and another. The line about the Fiesta was pure fiction. But I did genuinely have the Jag's number. It was getting latish now but I went down from the penthouse to the transport section and got connected to DVLC. I said I had an official enquiry on behalf of 6D2 and wheels were set in orbit pronto. After a minimal delay I discovered that my fiction had come very close to truth: the Jag's registration had belonged to a car that had been reported broken up. Not a Fiesta, but another Ford model, a Granada. I asked the name of the reporting garage or scrap dealer or whatever. I was given the name of a garage in Bristol. Proprietor Percy Excrudd.

Percy Excrudd could be worth a visit. Also, it might be a good idea to start right away. I could reach Bristol during the night, and the night would be a good time for a nice, quiet recce.

If there was a contact in the meantime it would be just too bad. I had a hunch that Percy Excrudd just might be of more value than just hanging about waiting for a phone call. In any case neither Brennan nor Ogmanfiller would, presumably, contact me again until they had instructions to pass, and it was early days for that. Largely, they were waiting for *me* to contact *them* with any helpful information I might glean. And in the meantime, Felicity would be okay. I hoped.

I took the BMW out of London onto the M4 motorway and the eventual intersection with the M32 that would take me right into Bristol. I had a working knowledge of the city; in my naval days I'd once been in a ship in Avonmouth and I and others used to drink in a pub and restaurant called the Mauretania: I'd heard since that it had been turned into a kind of club. But I could get my bearings from the Mauretania or from the university buildings at the top of the hill. Bristol I remembered as a traffic nightmare in daytime; at night it was easy though there was still some activity around. My road map of Bristol was somewhat out-of-date, but I found Percy Excrudd's establishment not far from where Bristol's principal tourist attraction, the SS *Great Britain*, was berthed in her dry-dock. PERCY EXCRUDD SCRAP METAL was blazoned over padlocked double doors giving access to a yard.

There was no one around. I sat and waited for a while, just to be sure. Then I got out and approached the big doors. I rattled the padlock which was secured to a heavy chain that held the doors together. If there had been, as I'd half expected, a guard dog behind the doors, then the rattle should have produced a reaction.

Nothing. Just a cat that appeared on top of the doors and then jumped down and rubbed itself against my legs. It rolled over for a tummy rub and I obliged. Satisfied, it went off down the road. The Excrudd premises were on a corner, and were enclosed by hoardings covered with adverts and graffiti. I moved round the corner, looking for some way of getting over the hoardings. I found it right at the end where the hoarding had deteriorated somewhat and more or less joined a low brick wall belonging to the neighbouring property that seemed to be a boatyard.

I got up on the wall and from there I was able to squeeze myself through a rotted section of the hoarding and drop down into the Excrudd domain.

There was scrap metal of all descriptions, junky stuff,

old refrigerators and cookers and washing machines, push-me-pull-you lawn mowers, rollers, wheelbarrows – and the remains of cars. Gutted chassis, exhaust systems, wheels, tow-bars. Two small cars awaiting attention, number plates gone.

Across the yard was what seemed to be the office building: just a shack, with two dirty windows either side of a door. The windows were largely covered with stickers – Castrol GTX, Duckhams, that sort of thing.

What I had come to find out were the particulars of the car that had shed its registration number in favour of the Jaguar. That, and more importantly the address of the Jag's owner.

I had, of course, to find out for myself: actually to make an enquiry would, supposing, as currently I had to, that Percy Excrudd was in cahoots with the Brennan-Ogmanfiller mob, rebound on Felicity. When Ogmanfiller got to hear, my snooping would scarcely fit my role of Trojan horse inside 6D2. Percy Excrudd might keep written records or he might not. If he did, they were likely to be somewhere in that shack.

I examined the locking arrangements on the door: a padlock again, not a particularly heavy one like that on the outside door, a hasp and staple. I was equipped for this and it didn't take me long – after I'd checked for a burglar alarm – to force the hasp away form the woodwork.

I went inside and used my pencil torch. A desk, two chairs, more junk and a cupboard, also locked but easily opened. First I went quickly through the drawers of the desk: nothing of interest there. Catalogues, handouts, free gift vouchers, some knitting that probably belonged to the office girl, a load of headed invoice forms and report sheets. In the centre drawer a cheque book and a packet of condoms along with Biros, pencils, rubbers and Tipp-Ex. Also a couple of spare nylon ribbons for a 'Brother' word processor.

I went to the cupboard. When I'd got it open I found more disappointment. It seemed to be nothing but a stationery cupboard, piled with more forms and invoices and stacks of paper and envelopes.

Not really too surprising: there would be a safe somewhere, maybe concealed beneath the floorboards. Or perhaps Percy Excrudd took the important stuff home at nights. The hot stuff, the incriminating stuff. If Percy Excrudd was on the fiddle. Which I reckoned he was.

So: first, the safe. If there was no safe, then I'd wasted my time. Or maybe not; a word with the boss in the morning might after all produce a little help. There were ways of asking questions that didn't give too much away.

I sounded round for loose floorboards; I examined the walls — the back wall of the shack wasn't wood, the building seemed to be built onto a cement-rendered wall, probably brick. I didn't find anything. I shifted a lurid calendar showing a nude girl reclining on a car bonnet, all flesh and high polish. There was nothing behind it.

When I turned away from the calendar I found I had

an audience of one. I hadn't heard a thing. But a very big man stood there, in the doorway, in my torch beam. He had to have the tread of a cat to carry that large frame plus stomach without making a sound.

We stared at one another.

I said, 'Mr Excrudd?'

He nodded. 'Right. You?'

'Ministry of Transport,' I said. 'Spot check.'

He jerked his head towards the road outside. 'That your BMW out there?'

I said it was.

'MOT inspectors don't get given BMWs.'

'You may have a point there,' I said coolly, 'but if I were you, I wouldn't send for the police. Just in case.'

He didn't like that. His face tightened up. He moved closer, and brought his hand out of the pocket where it had been stowed this far. He was holding a nasty-looking cosh, obviously very flexible and heavily lead-weighted. He asked, 'What are you looking for, friend?'

'I said, I'm MOT. If you've nothing to hide, you've nothing to get anxious about. I'd like to see your records.'

'What of?'

'Business,' I said. 'Purchases. Reports to DVLC . . . if you get my meaning.'

He came closer. I could feel his breath hot on my face. I saw a nasty red glint in rather piggy eyes. I saw the cosh come up and I reacted fast. I kneed him in the crutch, hard. As he gave a yelp and doubled up, I hit out. My aim was his jaw but his stomach got in the way of my fist and totally absorbed the force of the blow. It didn't seem to discommode him at all; and he was straightening, his face streaming with sweat. I didn't even see the cosh move. All I was aware of was a blinding flash of light and a momentary agony and then, I suppose, I went out flat.

I don't know how long I was out, but when I came to I found I was lying on a bed. I knew I was alive even though I felt like death. When I opened my eyes — and then very quickly closed them again — I felt a coolness on my forehead and water ran down my face. A voice said, speaking to someone else, 'He's coming round.' And then to me: 'Just lie still. You're going to be all right.'

A girl's voice.

A little water was tipped into my mouth and then I went out again. When, I don't know how long after, I opened my eyes once more I found I was able to keep them open and I saw that the girl was a nurse.

So I was in hospital. I felt as though I needed to be, but I wondered how and why.

Sitting on a hard chair by my bedside was a uniformed police constable.

I asked what went on.

The policeman didn't answer the question. He asked, 'Feeling better, are we?'

'Not noticeably,' I said. 'Just — tell me what happened, will you?'

He still wasn't giving anything away. He was
evidently the strong, silent type. Or he was acting under
orders. Things began to come back to me. The
scrapyard, the office shack, the office girl's knitting, the
packet of condoms, the sudden appearance of Percy
Excrudd – the cosh, the blinding light. But why was I
in hospital, why hadn't Percy Excrudd finished the job,
how did the police come into it?

And had I in any way compromised Felicity? All
manner of things crowded my mind, tumbling over each
other: the whip, Steenie Ogmanfiller, Polecat Brennan,
the two journeys in the Jag, my fast drive to Bristol,
Hedge and his stupid waffling, the schoolgirl, 'fuckin'
feet' and the hippie with the guitar, and Felicity again.
And, of course, Max.

Max was going to have my guts for garters.

Anyway, to cut my meanderings short: when I had
been passed fit enough for discharge by the medical
consultant, I was driven to police HQ. I was put in an
interview room and at once I asked to speak to the
officer in charge.

A plain-clothes man had entered the interview room
with me. He said, 'You won't need the chief super. Just
a few questions. It'll be referred up if necessary.'

I knew they'd already have my name: as in the case of
Ogmanfiller and her nasty little setup, I'd been left with
my notecase and other personal items: those, the constable at my bedside would have gone through for sure.

I said, 'I'm not answering anything until I've spoken
to your chief. Right?'

'Not right,' the plain-clothes man said. He said it civilly; he seemed a decent sort and I wasn't necessarily a villain, just a victim, but naturally he'd be keeping an open mind on that for the time being. 'I need to know what went on, now don't I?'

He invited me to sit down; I remained standing. I said, '6D2. You've heard of that? I'm with 6D2.'

He was surprised, I could see that. But his reaction told me he'd heard of 6D2, all right. He said, 'Well, well. You can prove that, I suppose?'

I said I could, once I was in touch with the chief superintendent.

'You'd better be telling the truth,' he said.

Focal House was contacted at once by telephone. After some talk and a bit of a wait I was handed the instrument. Max was on the line in person. He sounded icy; one way and another I was not surprised.

'What are you doing in Bristol, Shaw?'

'Making a contact. Or trying to.'

'I told you to keep in touch. That meant keeping me informed of your movements. Get back here pronto.'

I tried. I said, 'I've not finished . . .'

'You heard what I said: get moving, Shaw.'

'The police – '

'I'll talk to the police.'

I handed the telephone back to the chief superintendent. When he was through with Max, he said I was free to go but first there were some things he had to know. There were things I had to know too so we had quite a talk. It appeared that a police mobile had picked up a car heading fast out of the city. It wasn't just that this car had been shattering the speed limit: the police driver had had a hunch there was more to it than that, and the car, a Saab, had been followed at breakneck speed, other mobiles had been called in by radio and the Saab had been forced to a stop. A man, armed, had got out. He'd used his gun, wounding two policemen and had then made his getaway, hopping it over a wall and getting lost in a maze of back streets down towards Avonmouth.

I had been discovered, flat out in the back of the Saab.

Simple, really. And very, very fortunate for me, of course.

'So who was the man?' the chief super asked.

'Percy Excrudd,' I said, and I saw that the name was known, though not necessarily in a criminal connection. I said, 'I'll have to obey 6D2 orders, of course. In the meantime I'd be glad if you'd get hold of Percy Excrudd's office records which may be at his home address. I assume, after that gunfire, you have enough on him to make a check?'

He nodded. He asked, 'What exactly do you want to know, Commander Shaw?'

I told him something but not the whole story. I said, 'I believe he's been flogging the registration numbers of cars reported to DVLC as scrapped. Any information along those lines would be welcome.' And I gave him the number worn by the Ogmanfiller Jag.

* * *

I was asked if I wanted anything to eat. The canteen, they said, was available. I certainly didn't feel like eating but I had a cup of strong, black coffee and that helped. Then I was driven to Percy Excrudd's premises, where the doors were now standing open, to pick up my car. I saw a police vehicle in the yard. My BMW was still parked, on double yellow lines, and even as I got out of the police car I saw a warden about to attach a ticket, but my police driver dealt with that one.

I headed back for London, Focal House, and whatever it was Max needed me so urgently for.

I hoped he'd got a lead to Felicity but I doubted it. Unless something had emerged via Ashley Gardens, Westminster. Following Cello Charlie's report of a sighting of Polecat Brennan, the Ashley Gardens area had been put under 6D2 surveillance, which was always very, very discreet and was largely carried out by means of telescopic lenses. There were plenty of vantage points around Ashley Gardens and the outfit's specialists would be peering closely into bedrooms and so on and if Polecat Brennan did show up there, he would be spotted for sure.

But I still didn't believe he'd take the risk. No flies on Polecat Brennan. Even they couldn't stand the stench of evil.

5

I was still desperately worried about pulling the wool over Max's eyes; I doubted if he would ever trust me again. There was still Felicity, but I was coming round to the big decision that I had to come clean with Max. He would know how to handle it in such a way that the villains never got to know I'd talked. Of course he would.

Wouldn't he?

Not necessarily.

I had plenty of past reasons to know that Polecat Brennan had ears and eyes everywhere, any number of plants and contacts. I'd not be surprised to find he had plants growing inside the outfit's networks, even inside Focal House itself — he already half had me and I had to face it.

Felicity came, of course, under the general heading of personal feelings. As such, she hadn't to count. That was an axiom. The first thing that was drummed into you in any service.

Could I, in the long run, go against my whole training, both in the RN and in 6D2? Could I, after a while, keep it up anyway? The truthful answer to that was no, I couldn't. Sooner or later I would tie myself in a knot and Max would rumble me and it would all come out. That wasn't going to be of much help to Felicity; nor to the French Foreign Minister. I would be acting against all sorts of interests: the European Community and Britain itself to name just two.

That I couldn't deny.

But.

There was still a 'but'.

I had to resolve this before I reached Focal House. I was split right in half.

The call came on my car telephone just as I was about to hit the intersection with the M25. Don't ask me how Polecat Brennan had got my number, but the caller was him all right.

He wanted to know how I was progressing.

I said, 'Nothing to report.'

'Is that so?' The tone was very nasty. 'You've been in Bristol. Why?'

'If you know I've been in Bristol,' I said, because there was no point in contradicting what obviously he did know, 'I'm sure you can find out the rest for yourself.'

I cut the call. Less than a minute later, back he came.

'Maybe I can,' he said, nastier than ever. 'But you're on a slippery slope. Or Miss Mandrake is. Don't you forget that.' This time it was Brennan who cut the call. I believe he was just issuing a warning, a reminder, and in fact he knew very well what I'd been doing in Bristol.

Percy Excrudd wouldn't have been slow to pass the word on his car phone, which of itself finally incriminated Percy Excrudd. I could only hope the Bristol police would get their hands on him. Before leaving the nick, I'd taken Max's name in vain, telling the chief superintendent that Focal House was to be informed of any arrest, and no questioning to take place until I or someone from Focal House was present. He'd agreed to that.

The M25 was busy; so were all the routes in central London. Max was in a foul mood when at last I reported to the penthouse suite.

He said, 'First thing: I want a full report on what you were after in Bristol.'

I told him. I really had no option now. I told him the whole thing to date. About the geographically unknown cellar, about Steenie Ogmanfiller, about the television – about Felicity. About what amounted to my own treachery.

Of course, he hit the roof. Having hit it, he remained kind of jammed there for a full vocal two minutes. Then he simmered down.

'You're all kinds of a bloody fool, Shaw,' he finished. 'But you know that, of course. I can only thank God you've come back to your sense of duty in time. Before any actual harm's been done.' He had got up from his desk during his rant, had been walking up and down the room, like an admiral on his quarterdeck. Now he stopped, turned his back and stared for a while out of one of his big windows, the one that looked across the helicopter landing pad outside the penthouse.

He said, still with his back to me, 'We may be able to turn this to some advantage. Right, Shaw?'

'You mean – feed back false information?'

'Exactly.'

'Brennan could be expecting that.'

'True, he could. But he won't be sure. And he's got that hold over you.'

'No need to remind me,' I said.

'You're a complete bloody ass,' Max said angrily. 'But it so happens I don't want to lose Miss Mandrake any more than you do.' He turned away from the window. 'We'll have a devil of a lot of covering up to do. For your peace of mind, I can assure you that nothing of what you've just told me will go further than this room – that's not because of you principally. It's because of the value I place on Miss Mandrake. I hope you're clear on that.'

'Clear,' I said. 'What about Hedge?'

'Oh, balls to Hedge. I'll keep him happy. Now I'd better tell you why I wanted you here.'

I was all agog. Max said, 'Pierre Monet. In case you've forgotten,' he added sarcastically, 'the French Foreign Minister.'

'Not forgotten.'

'You surprise me.' Max was still sore. 'His visit's been brought forward. That's to remain top secret right the way through until he arrives in London and our man arrives in Paris.' By 'our man' I took it he meant the Foreign Secretary. 'No chances are being taken – the

threat has got London and Paris in a real tizzy, of
course.'

'So when's he due now?'

'The whole thing's been advanced twenty-four
hours.'

So we now had just six days. Six days to inhibit
Polecat Brennan's mob. Six days for Felicity.
Uppermost in my mind was the urgency of getting her
out from under before Pierre Monet and our Foreign
Secretary did their crossover act. Once it dawned on
Brennan that the mat had been slid from under him, I
wouldn't give much for Felicity's chances of staying
alive. Revenge had always been high on Polecat
Brennan's list of priorities.

I didn't mention this to Max in so many words. He
would know it for himself, and I'd already leaned too
heavily in the Felicity direction. From now on out my
target had to be Pierre Monet's safety. That before
anything else. Before I left, Max told me that he'd
found no more information on Louis X or von
Defflinger-Zwickau than had Hedge. Except that there
were Defflinger-Zwickau factories in various parts of
Germany, making industrial machinery. Very respectable. Hedge had probably made a cockup.

There had been nothing through from Bristol by the
time I left Focal House. Leaving, I thought about
Ashley Gardens. I was mightily tempted to go along to
that flat and take a look at what might be there. Max
had confirmed that the telescopic-lens viewers had seen

nothing, that the flat appeared to be totally empty. But it didn't have to be empty of clues and leads, I thought. On the other hand, it would most probably not be long before Brennan got to know that I'd been there snooping and that would be of no help to anyone.

Best leave it. Leave it and wait. I'd known all along that this had to some extent to be a waiting game. But I couldn't wait too long. Soon, something would have to be stirred up.

Well, I would wait until Polecat Brennan made another telephone contact.

He − or rather this time Steenie Ogmanfiller − made it as I was driving along past Knightsbridge Barracks on the way to my flat.

'You've been in Focal House,' she stated.

I asked, 'How come you know all my movements?'

'Don't ask,' she said. There was a pause. 'You'll have something to tell us,' she said.

'Will I?'

'Miss Mandrake's relying on you,' the Ogmanfiller said meaningly.

'Yes. Well.' I gathered my thoughts together again − the reminder, however unnecessary it had been, had temporarily scattered things in my mind. Thoughts gathered, I went on. 'The threat's being taken seriously − the politicians are worried.'

'Yes, okay. So − ?'

I said, 'I can't say any more on the phone. You should realize that for yourself.'

'But − '

'No,' I told her. 'Positively no. I'm putting myself at risk as it is. I could go down for treason. We'll have to meet.'

'I can't – '

'Listen,' I said, 'there's no other way.'

'But you – '

'No other way,' I said with emphasis. 'Absolutely no other way.'

There was a sound of annoyance and worry. 'I'll ring again,' Ogmanfiller said, and cut the call. I imagined the acne flaming all over her face, the angry movement of her more-or-less non-existent breasts. She wouldn't like being in a cleft stick, but she was going to have to put up with it or risk losing some vital information. I knew she, or Brennan, would ring back with a rendezvous. Soon after I got to the flat, the line from Focal House burred. Bristol police had caught up with Percy Excrudd who was being held incommunicado for questioning as soon as someone from 6D2 arrived.

'Tell them I'll be down myself,' I said, 'soonest possible.' Brennan or Ogmanfiller could call me en route if they chose; my whereabouts wouldn't make any difference to that.

So – back to Bristol. A lot would now depend on Percy Excrudd, on whether or not he could be broken down. Quickly. I was becoming very conscious of time going past. I thought, as I drove out of London, about Ogmanfiller. I was going to tell her, when that meeting was arranged as it would be, that Pierre Monet might be coming over by air. Or even the ferry, or the hovercraft or whatever to Folkestone. Leaving them with a little bit of guesswork certainly wouldn't come amiss. I thought also about the facts as given me by Max, the twenty-four-hour difference.

How were the authorities going to maintain secrecy on that?

I imagined Hedge getting in a real tizzy. Hedge struck me as the sort of pompous man who would set great store by strict protocol, by bullshit, to give it a more accurate name. What about the red carpet at the London terminal, the Captain's Escort of the Household Cavalry, the carriages, the royal personage who would represent the Queen, the stationmaster, all the rest of the appendages essential to State visits, the equerries, the police who would have to clear the route, all that sort of thing?

No secrecy there; bullshit called for a hell of a lot of preparation that couldn't help but be overt. Even the grooms and the horses. They couldn't be turned on at the flick of a finger. Nor could secrecy be maintained even if it was a more-or-less anonymous arrival by a little man like Hedge, in black coat and striped trousers, bowler hat and umbrella, and no fanfare of trumpets. No politician can ever be totally anonymous; the press sees to that.

And Ogmanfiller? Just how had she known I'd been in Focal House? Did that indicate a mole inside 6D2 HQ Britain? Possibly. On the other hand I could have been followed. On another hand, and a likely enough one, it could have been an intelligent guess. Focal House would be a natural for a visit ex-Bristol.

In the Bristol nick I had a preliminary word with the chief superintendent.

'Stroppy,' he said in reference to Percy Excrudd. 'Song and dance routine about what do we think we're at. Demands for his solicitor to be present — after all, it's his right, anyway once the questioning starts.'

'No solicitor,' I said.

'As I said, it's his right, Commander.'

'No solicitor,' I said again. 'I'll take full responsibility for that.'

I was taken to the interview room where Percy Excrudd was being held. He was physically big as I'd had occasion to note at close quarters the night before. Seen fully in the bright light of the interview room — electric light, since dark was coming down now — he looked highly unpleasant. A big red face with protruding lower lip, pig's eyes, truculent expression now overlaid with a mouth-twisting sneer. I noted his hands, too: they were boxer's hands, bruiser's hands.

He looked at me. 'The man from the Ministry of Transport,' he said. 'The phoney inspector. What's all this about, then?'

I said, 'Just a few enquiries to assist the police.'

'Who're you, then?'

I said, 'We won't go into that.' He might know who I was from information received via Polecat Brennan or he might not. I was going to leave it that way for now.

'If you've got anything on me, or if you think you

have, go ahead and bloody charge me,' Excrudd said. 'But not before I'm allowed my rights to have my solicitor present.'

I disposed of that one, though not without potential trouble. Percy Excrudd got suddenly to his feet and gesticulated towards me across the table. That didn't last; a plain-clothes man standing behind Excrudd put a heavy hand on each of his shoulders and forced him back down onto the chair.

I said, 'Right. Now the questions. They refer to your business. As a scrap-metal merchant I mean.'

The pig eyes became furtive: did I, they seemed to be registering, know about any other business?

'A question of disposal of scrapped cars. That, and the consequent reports to DVLC. I have a particular interest in registration numbers. If you follow.'

'I don't follow, no.'

'I rather think you do, Mr Excrudd. I rather think you have sources of income aside from your business, your legitimate business.' The chief superintendent had told me Percy Excrudd's address: it was in a very fashionable, very expensive suburb. Excrudd had a wife who liked expensive furs, and he had two children at expensive private schools. Apart from the Saab, he also owned a Ford Granada, a Range Rover and a powerboat, not a big one but costly enough.

'My bloody income, that's my affair.'

'There are times, and this is one of them, when it becomes a matter of public interest, Mr Excrudd,' I said smoothly.

He glared at me. 'You the bloody bloodsuckers then?
Is that what this is?'

'If you refer to the Inland Revenue,' I said, 'then I'm
not one of them. As I think you very well know, don't
you, Mr Excrudd? I told you, my interest lies in car
registration numbers. That's all.' I paused. 'I have
reason to believe you're involved in selling off
registrations of scrapped cars — to persons who make
use of them for criminal purposes. Would you care to
comment on that, Mr Excrudd?'

'No, I wouldn't. Except to say that's all bloody
bollocks. You've nothing on me, nothing at all — '

'Oh, but if I were you, I wouldn't be too sure of that,'
I interrupted. Then I quoted at him the registration
number of the Jaguar. 'Does that ring a bell?' I asked.

'No,' he said flatly. Well, of course, he might not
carry all his business dealings in his head — fair enough,
though I believed he'd remember that number well
enough. I nudged his memory.

I said, 'You know Polecat Brennan. Don't you, Mr
Excrudd?'

That went home in a somewhat spectacular way.
Percy Excrudd got to his feet again as suddenly as
before. Before he could be stopped he'd heaved the
table up and tipped it onto me and the chief
superintendent who was standing beside me. The police
officer went down, taken totally by surprise. I heaved
the table back at Percy Excrudd, more or less — he'd
shifted by this time, and a uniformed constable was
grabbing for him. He was brought under control,

handcuffs were with some difficulty slid onto his wrists and he was plumped back onto the hard chair.

'It seems we've gone some way towards an admission,' I said. 'Now I'm going to bring a few strands together. I want an address, Mr Excrudd, and believe you me, I'm going to get it. Never you think otherwise.'

Excrudd's face had gone almost purple. He began to pant. It looked like a heart attack but it wasn't. It was sheer rage; that, and fear. It was the fear I had to work on, the fear not only of the police and what their investigations might do to his lifestyle, but fear also of Polecat Brennan. The latter, I fancied, was the more potent. At least the Old Bill wouldn't kill him.

So that was the fear I played on.

Polecat Brennan, I said, was a very vicious man. He had many quite clever ways of disposing of unwanted persons. When anyone had dealings with Polecat Brennan, they were well advised to take out life insurance. Not financial life insurance, but physical life insurance. In other words, protection. Guaranteed protection.

I could offer that, I said. He'd already virtually committed himself to knowing Polecat Brennan; and I knew he'd done business with him. From Polecat Brennan's point of view, that guaranteed retribution to come if and when things went wrong. There couldn't be the slightest doubt about that. The retribution would be nasty and wouldn't necessarily bc confined to the pig-eyed Percy: there were the wife and children. Polecat

Brennan would be merciless: the mere fact that Percy Excrudd had got himself into police hands would be enough for Polecat Brennan to start the process, I said. I could see he believed me.

'And all I want is an address,' I said. 'That's all. After that, you're safe though I can't speak for the police. That is, you could face prosecution. Then again maybe not. If you're willing to help, it'll go in your favour. But I'll guarantee your immunity from Polecat Brennan just so long as we get to him in time. And we'll do that if you give us that address I'm after. Polecat Brennan will be put away for a very, very long time. It's entirely up to you. I suggest you think about it, Mr Excrudd.'

Percy Excrudd licked away at dry lips, his face ghastly now. I believe he was seeing all manner of nasty deaths. After a while, he said, 'If I tell you — do I get protection right away?'

'Right away,' I told him.

'How?'

I caught the eye of the chief superintendent and I said, 'Helping the police with their enquiries. Become resident for a while. How about that?'

He agreed. Anything was better than Polecat Brennan. He asked, what about his family? The chief super dealt with that: there would be police protection round the clock. That seemed to satisfy Percy Excrudd. He gave me the address. I'd half feared it was going to turn out to be Ashley Gardens, which wouldn't be news and wouldn't be a lot of help. But it wasn't. It was an address in Cambridgeshire, in the fens. Maybe that accounted for the dankness of that cellar.

I called Max on the security line from the nick. I passed the address given by Percy Excrudd.

'And you?' Max asked.

I knew what he meant. 'I'm going in,' I said. 'Time's short, as we know.'

'Back-up?'

Again I knew what he meant: the heavy mob. But I didn't want that yet. I said, 'No. First thing's a recce. If necessary, I'll contact later.'

'Watch it,' Max said. For the third time I knew what he meant: Miss Mandrake wasn't to be my first consideration. I had to smash the threat, ensure a nice, safe arrival for Pierre Monet. Having issued that veiled warning, Max cut the call. I took my leave of the chief superintendent and once again drove out of Bristol, this time to head into the fens north of Ely.

6

It was a long drive through the night. I stopped for petrol and a meal at a service station on the M4, then I hit the M25 for the M11 and on to the A10 north of Cambridge. It was a little south of Ely that my car phone rang and I heard the Ogmanfiller voice announcing the expected rendezvous for the imparting of information.

'Piccadilly Underground station,' she said, and I thought of Hedge.

'When?'

'How soon can you get there?'

I thought fast. I doubted if they had any idea where I was at that moment. I knew I hadn't had a tail. I asked, 'How soon can *you* get there?'

'When you do.'

Suits me, I thought: Ogmanfiller must be in London, which meant one fewer to deal with. Also it meant that they would never expect me to turn up at the hideout, so if after my recce I decided to go in, the surprise would be total. I said, 'Okay, be seeing you in half an hour.'

'No tricks,' Ogmanfiller said.

'No tricks.'

'Or else.'

That was all. The voice of Steenie Ogmanfiller fell silent on that nasty note. When I didn't turn up at the rendezvous I could have been mugged en route, I could have met with a nasty road accident, I could have been pushed under a tube train — *could* have, no exaggeration in today's great metropolis. But I didn't really believe I'd be given the benefit of the doubt. Or rather that Felicity would be.

But, of course, I hadn't to think of Felicity. Only of Pierre Monet. And the EC.

I drove on. The address was that of, I presumed, a private dwelling. It was in a village, which I'd found as no more than a dot on my road map, on an unclassified road — a village named Lower Downham. Not far from Downham Market and the Denver Sluice that I believed regulated the water-flow, or maybe stopped the water-flow, of various rivers so that they didn't inundate the reclaimed fenland. The further I went north of Cambridge the bleaker the landscape became. An immensity of sky as I could see when the moon came brilliantly out from behind cloud cover. A lonely, dyke-crossed land, with an east wind blowing now. Totally flat, with Ely Cathedral standing out like an immense finger pointing skywards, a sight that would be visible for very many miles across the fens.

A few miles south of Downham Market I picked up the signpost for Lower Downham, a right-hand turn. Seeing that road sign I was reminded of another road sign, down in Hampshire south of Winchester: Higher

Upham. That had tickled my sense of humour at the time; but there was no humour around tonight. God alone knew what I was about to stick my neck into. And all I had was my shoulder-holstered Biretta. That, and a little gadget hidden away, a tiny radio transmitter that I'd picked up from the flat that morning – correction, yesterday morning now – and could come in handy should I want the heavies sent in. It was a small enough armoury; but I thought back to what I'd heard about the last war. We'd not had enough ships or guns or tanks or aircraft but we'd pulled through in the end. So they'd said. I didn't think myself that we'd really pulled through all that well into the present day. Not now that the EC had thrust Britain into the jaws of Germany and France. I didn't want to be a European.

Nevertheless, I drove on to act for Europe. Hedge's Europe; I was sure that pompous little cretin found it expedient to appear a good European.

The snow started just as I came to the outskirts of Lower Downham. That cloud had closed in and was now at full sky cover, doing away with the moon. The snowfall was very heavy and got quickly heavier. I switched my wipers on to full lick but it didn't help; they just clogged up. I drove dead slow, getting such bearing as I could before the snow made everything anonymous. The address prised out of Percy Excrudd was The Moorings, 76 High Street. High Street had to be the road I was currently on. There didn't seem to be any other roads, at least not until I came to a crossroads with signs pointing to Ely one way, Downham Market the other.

I kept ahead, sticking to what I had to assume was the extension of the High Street.

Then I stopped. There was a clump of trees at what seemed to be the end of the village proper. The Moorings could be outside the actual village – probably was, had to be, what with the comings and goings of Polecat Brennan's mob, and that cellar and all. Not the kind of setup to site plonk in a village centre with all the inevitability of gossip. A big house outside and apart from the immediate village would be different: these days, all sorts of weirdos inhabited the big houses whose original owners hadn't the money to keep them up and had been forced to surrender to the scrap-iron merchants, the stars of pop or football – and the Polecat Brennans.

I started up again and moved into the clump of trees, pulling off the road. Just before I switched off the engine, my car phone called me again. Did I answer or did I not? It was almost certainly Ogmanfiller. But it could be Focal House.

I didn't answer. If Ogmanfiller suspected something she wouldn't know what, and Piccadilly Underground was a long way from Lower Downham.

With the car well hidden from casual sight, I got out, locked the doors and started on the recce.

I found the house, or anyway a house, about a mile farther on. Not having seen it on my earlier visit, thanks to bags over heads and so on, I naturally didn't recognize it. And come to that, it didn't have to be the same house. Polecat Brennan could have a number of addresses. But I had a hunch it was the same house.

I went forward, cautiously. There was a ditch, or dyke, currently with no more than a slop of water in it – East Anglia had been suffering a winter drought, until now anyway. That snow was going to melt eventually. The dyke ran past the drive to the house; there was a miniature bridge giving access. I dropped down into the slop of water. I was already whitened by the snow, which had become a blizzard, and I moved rather like a ghost, pretty well invisible being the same colour as my surroundings.

I saw the name on a board fastened to a gatepost: The Moorings. Whether or not it was the house with the cellar and the TV, it was the house named by Percy Excrudd.

Now what?

Watch and wait? A watch could go on indefinitely and I couldn't risk the light of day, obviously. So I left the dyke's cover and moved inside the gate. There was a hedge running to right and left of the gateway; I slunk along to the left, keeping below the top of the hedge, a mobile snowball heading for the back of the house. I saw the integral garage and that fitted with my previous arrival and though, of course, The Moorings wouldn't be the only house with an integral garage I still had that hunch and felt I'd hit the target.

It was late now and there were no lights to be seen, though there could be wakefulness behind thick curtains for all I knew. I approached the back of the house, coming close up to a window. I tried to peer through and I found just blankness, one of those thick curtains . . . then I heard, faintly, the ring of a telephone.

I didn't like that. Ogmanfiller, ringing from Piccadilly Underground to report my non-arrival, an indication to The Moorings that something had come adrift?

Could be.

The ringing went on. Then I saw through a chink of the curtain that a light had come on behind the window. More than that I couldn't see, and, of course, I couldn't hear the conversation when the ringing stopped.

After about a minute the light went out. There being nothing else to do, I waited to see what happened next. What happened next was a surprise. Another light came on, away to my left − I saw the stream of sudden brilliance lighting up the garden. I shifted berth; the lit-up window was over a staircase, on a half-landing. Climbing the stairs was a clergyman, an old man with a dog collar and a black dickie, none of this modern colouring, blue, grey or what-have-you.

Why, for heaven's sake, a clergyman? Had Percy Excrudd been pulling the wool, or what? I doubted rather strongly that he had; too easy, obviously, to be bowled out with nasty consequences for Percy Excrudd.

My hunch still held; this was the house.

Why the parson, the pillar of respectability?

I stayed where I was. Soon, the clergyman came down

again, and as he descended I heard a loud, shrill voice, female and angry. 'Just you bloody watch it, Fred,' the voice yelled down the stairs. 'Could be a trap, right?'

'Piss off, can't you,' the clergyman shouted back. 'Got to do the part.'

'Bloody parishioners!' the voice yelled, then there was the sound of a door being slammed, hard. The parson continued down the stairs. He was now wearing an overcoat: deduction, he was going out. To do something in connection with a bloody parishioner? Last rites maybe?

I was bewildered. I moved back to the side of the house as the light over the stairs was switched off. I heard stirrings in the integral garage, a door being opened and then shut again, the outer door being lifted from inside. The clergyman drove out into the blizzard, out over the bridge, and turned right for the village.

The angry female voice had yelled out something about a trap.

Why a trap for an elderly parson going upon his errand of mercy? And again, why a parson anyway?

It didn't add up.

Or did it?

If this was Polecat Brennan's hideout – and the strident woman within didn't sound to me like the usual rector's wife . . . .

I have a fair imagination, and I used it, building a scenario while I pondered the next move. Let's say the clergyman is a fake. A clergyman of any sort, even fake provided he doesn't get found out, would be good cover. The best, in fact. The pillar of respectability again. On the other hand, it would be easy to be found out. But not so easy if the parson knew his stuff, knew how to cope with, say, the last rites. So this parson might have been in fact ordained, in full possession of a pulpit-keeping certificate as it were.

And he might have lost it along the way. He might have transgressed, he might have been defrocked or anyway chucked out of his living for some nasty sin, a sin that might have involved the female possessor of the strident voice. If such was the case, then I wouldn't expect him to have been appointed rector of the parish, or joined parishes in these days of a shortage of priests. But he could act as a stand-in when required, when the rector was away, or sick, or just too tired to get out of bed in a blizzard. Send for Fred, the official incumbent's wife might have said, Fred'll do it. Good old Fred, likes to keep his hand in.

He could get away with that sort of thing. His record would not have been gone into too closely. Willing Freds were not to be made to open their mouths for inspection like gift horses. They were worth their weight in gold.

Very handy for Polecat Brennan. Evil didn't lurk in the sanctity of parsons' homes.

It was all in my mind, no more than that, but it added up.

In the meantime there was no Ogmanfiller. And now The Moorings held one less person. And next time the phone went, it could well be Ogmanfiller, waiting in

Piccadilly unless they'd chased her out by now. Anyway, there was always a phone somewhere.

It was time to go in and take a look.

Going in was easier said than done.

Someone in that house was security-minded. All the windows were immovable, fitted no doubt with all kinds of locks. Also the doors, back and front, plus the one leading indoors from the integral garage.

But the garage was the best bet. The parson had to return some time or other. I would wait for that. In the meantime I went back into cover, close up to the hedge. The snow continued; I estimated a couple of inches already, and it was coming down so thick that it was deadening sound and not making seeing very easy either. And it was beginning to drift on a keen easterly wind. East Anglia, the fens in particular, was a very exposed area. The wind came probably straight from Siberia.

Did I use my tiny transmitter and warn Focal House?

Not yet, I decided. I had a lot to find out first; to have the heavies around might muck things up. I wasn't ready yet. I didn't want to flush anything out until I was. So I didn't use the transmitter, which was perhaps a pity as things were to turn out.

I waited, growing icy cold. Then, at last, I heard the crunch of a car approaching through the deepening snowfall. Hearing that sound, I made it fast into the garage, concealing myself as best I could behind a side pillar. I didn't intend to find myself shut out if the parson operated the door too suddenly.

As it happened, he didn't get that far. Not just then.

I heard a nasty crunch. I looked round the pillar: the car stood stopped and somewhat askew just the other side of the bridge over the dyke. Its bonnet had hit the bridgework and the nearside front wheel was hanging over the dyke. No chains, I thought. Lack of proper preparation.

Then I heard the angry voice. 'Sod the bugger.'

Unparsonic.

I came out from the garage, my hand ready to bring out the Biretta. I approached the parson. I asked, 'Can I help?'

He hadn't seen me till now, hadn't heard my approach. He swung round. 'Well, I'll be bu—' The tone changed. 'Bless my soul! Where have you come from . . . my dear fellow?'

'Up the road,' I said.

'I didn't see you.'

'The local snowman,' I said easily. 'Hard to pick out on a night like this.'

'You don't sound local like.'

The voice was reverting, temporary culture slipping away. I didn't believe he was a parson at all, not even a defrocked one. And for his part he was getting suspicious. I remembered the voice, warning him the call-out might be a trap. I believe that was what he, too, was remembering. I pressed it home. I said, 'She did warn you, Fred,' and as I said that I brought the Biretta into view. And in view it was, from the courtesy light that had come on in the car when the parson had opened the door.

'What the fuck — '

Once again it just didn't go with the clerical collar, even though times had changed and the priesthood, or anyway the younger ones, had changed with them. I said, 'Into the house. Leave the car.'

'I — '

'Just do as I say. Do it fast and do it circumspectly. No yelling for help. Who else is in the house, Fred?'

'What's it to you, eh?'

'Quite a lot. Who else? The lady I know about. Who else?'

'No one.'

'Not Polecat Brennan?'

His reaction gave certain facts away: he knew Polecat Brennan, I reckoned. But he didn't say so. He said, 'I don't know what you're on about.'

I grinned. 'We'll find out, shall we? Into the house for a start, right?'

We went in through the garage. I told Fred to shut the garage door behind us and he did so. In the light that he switched on as we came through into the house I was able to take a good look at him. His face was heavy, lowering and now glowering, and the bluish nose and veined cheeks gave evidence of much drink consumed over his perhaps sixty-odd years. He was heavily built, bull-like, and he had crafty eyes. Nevertheless, there was something about him that told me he could play the parson fairly convincingly when he kept his mind on the act. Maybe it was just the clerical outfit – I don't know. What I did know now was that I was definitely *not* in the house where I'd been taken originally: different layout.

Just after the light was switched on, a woman appeared, descending the stairs. In a nightdress that showed a good deal of bosom; she was a buxom piece, aged around forty at a guess and not bad-looking in a blowsy sort of way. Seeing us she put a hand to her mouth and said around it, 'Well, I never! Who's this, Fred?'

'Dunno. Got a gun 'e 'as.'

'Is he – '

'I said, I dunno.'

He looked all set to have a go at me. If he did, I would use the Biretta. Just a winging shot. The woman came slowly down, breathing heavily. I decided that Polecat Brennan was not in residence. For my money, if he'd been there, he'd have shown by now.

As the woman reached the bottom of the stairs, the telephone rang. This time it was bound to be Ogmanfiller. I said, 'I'll take it.' I gestured to the woman. 'You'll come with us,' I said. 'Don't try anything.'

They went ahead of the Biretta, into the room where the telephone was. I wondered why Ogmanfiller hadn't rung while the parson was out, but evidently she hadn't or the woman would have said. On the other hand she might not have done in my presence.

I took up the receiver. I didn't identify myself.

It wasn't Ogmanfiller. A man's voice said, 'Shift of plan. I'm coming down.'

That was all. The voice was Polecat Brennan's. I'd hit one target, all right, even if this wasn't the original house.

The woman asked shrilly, 'Who was that, then?'

'Someone for me,' I said.

I saw the look that passed between the woman and Fred. They didn't know whether or not to believe me, but if I was speaking the truth then my presence in the house was obviously known elsewhere and that wouldn't be too good for them. If I wasn't speaking the truth, then they'd missed out on something and only I knew what.

Either way, they didn't like it.

As for me, Polecat Brennan was on the way in. How long before he arrived remained a mystery. I would have to be in all respects ready to receive him. And it was still not the time to alert Focal House. The heavies were pretty good at self-concealment but I wasn't taking any risks now. This was, in the first instance, to be between me and Polecat Brennan and no way would I chance having him scared off before he was inside the house.

I smiled at Fred and the woman. I said, 'How about a nice cup of tea? And perhaps a little talk about the church, h'm? But first I'd like you to show me over the house.'

We went over it room by room. There was no sign of Felicity. We ended the tour in the kitchen. There was an electric cooker, an electric kettle. The woman made tea from bags, one to each of three cups. During the brewing I thought about Steenie Ogmanfiller and her long wait, now presumably ended, in Piccadilly Underground station. Polecat Brennan had spoken of a shift in the plan, whatever the plan might be. I fancied this would have to do with my non-arrival at the rendezvous. Ogmanfiller had probably contacted Brennan direct when I'd finally failed to show.

The woman slapped the mugs down on the bare kitchen table. 'I bloody hope it poisons you,' she said viciously. 'Just who are you, eh?'

I thought the time had come to put a few cards on the table. I said, 'I'm an investigator.'

'Oh, yes? Into what, might I ask?'

'Polecat Brennan,' I said. 'Not a nice person. Not for the Church to be associated with. Wouldn't you agree, Padre? When you really come to think deeply about it.'

Fred muttered something I didn't catch. I said, 'Something tells me you two are very peripheral.'

'Perry what?' the woman asked.

'Oh, never mind. I mean, you're kind of on the fringe of events. Just being used by Polecat Brennan. You might be able to do yourselves some good by answering a few questions.' I wanted desperately to ask about Felicity; but I was holding back since something was telling me it was better that way until I had Brennan in front of my gun and I was able to contact Focal House for a pick-up. 'For instance: how committed are you to the Church, Fred?'

'Come off it,' Fred said uneasily.

'Off what?' I asked, all innocence.

'The bloody Church bit.' Fred had seen that that was blown.

'You mean you're not a clerk in Holy Orders?'

'Bloody heck as like.'

Well, that was a start. An idea struck me. I put it into words. I asked, 'Have you ever done any acting, Fred?'

He said yes, he had. BBC, radio plays, not TV. Provincial theatres plus end-of-pier stuff. Blackpool, Bridlington, Skegness and Minehead, the last two being holiday camps – he wasn't on the higher rungs of the profession. Worthing, Brighton, Eastbourne, Hastings – Folkestone.

Folkestone.

'That where you met Polecat Brennan?' I asked casually. 'Folkestone?'

He wasn't admitting to knowing Polecat Brennan. I read into that that he wasn't expecting Brennan to show at The Moorings. He was thus in for a shock.

'Did you ever,' I asked, 'play religious parts?'

He said, yes he had. He expanded a little. Mostly comic characters, vicars in compromising situations involving trousers that fell down, that sort of thing, and women, not the sort of women that vicars normally associated with. At this point the buxom woman giggled, but only briefly. Fred went on. He'd also played serious church roles. Once he'd been a dean; that was on the BBC.

He didn't say much more but once again I tried to

build up a scenario and failed. Polecat Brennan obviously had a use for this fenland house even though it didn't contain Felicity. I couldn't guess at the use Brennan was putting the house to, but it seemed he'd needed cover by way of Fred in his serious-parsonic, respectable role. And he'd probably not needed the cover for very long; Pierre Monet was within days of death. After that, these two would be expendable.

They probably hadn't been told that yet.

Outside, the blizzard continued without any let-up. Unless he arrived very soon, Brennan wasn't going to make it, not even on foot. The east wind howled, banshee-like, building up the drifts. The kitchen was already cold and it grew colder. This was the sort of house, and the sort of district, that called loudly for an Aga for cook to sit by, anyway in the days of cook; then, there would undoubtedly have been a kitchen range, coal-fired, spreading warmth and comfort around cook nodding off in a big basketwork chair.

Making conversation while I awaited Polecat Brennan, feeling that if we built up some sort of camaraderie something might emerge that wasn't meant to, I talked of kitchen ranges. Had there once been one here, did they think?

'Dunno.' They just weren't interested; they had more weighty matters on their minds.

I jerked the Biretta towards a wall where there was a large sheet of what looked like hardboard slotted against the wall and held by runners. It could be covering a recess – an empty recess where once had stood the kitchen range.

'It could have been over there,' I said.

No response; but I noted a sudden change in the atmosphere, a kind of tautening of nerves and an avoidance of Fred and the woman catching each other's eye. Also, their faces had tightened up. I'd hit something but as yet I didn't know what. I got to my feet and, keeping the Biretta trained on the two of them, I approached the hardboard. I gave it a tap; there was a hollow sound. Another tap, a harder one, produced more hollow sounds. A gap behind, as I'd thought, where the kitchen range had been removed.

Nothing much in that. Or wouldn't have been if they hadn't reacted in the somewhat negative way they had.

It was worth investigating further. I was about to do so when I heard other sounds, sounds from outside. Someone pushing his way through snow? Moments later I heard a key turning in a door, the back door. It opened and closed again. I kept the Biretta trained on Fred and the woman, getting them between me and the kitchen door so that I was covering all eventualities.

The kitchen door opened and Polecat Brennan came in.

7

I'd not seen Brennan in the flesh for a few years, but he hadn't changed much. The same sallow face, the shifty eyes, the thick bruiser's body, the vicious slit of a mouth, the overall hard look of a man who would, and did, kill without thought when it suited him. A man who was power mad and had not a drop of humanity in his veins, his head or his heart. A heartless man.

With the ridiculous fake parson and the blowsy woman there had been almost a degree of comedy. There was no comedy now; just the hard reality of a monster.

Brennan was shaken rigid at seeing me there in the kitchen of his safe house. I had the advantage for the time being. My hand was ready with the Biretta. If Brennan had shown the slightest movement of his own hands, I'd have dropped him on the spot. He knew that.

He licked at his lips. 'So, Commander Shaw,' he said. 'What brings you here?'

'Pierre Monet,' I said. 'As if you didn't know.'

He smiled coldly, a polecat's smile if polecats ever smiled. 'Or Miss Mandrake, perhaps?'

'Perhaps. Where is she, Brennan?'

'You would so much like to know! Well, let us be sensible and talk together. Let us be – civilized.' There was nothing civilized about Polecat Brennan, never had been. 'I have what you want. You have what I want.'

'What do you want, Brennan?'

'Knowledge. Information. Let me remind you, that was what you agreed to provide. So that Miss Mandrake would not be ill-treated. Do you remember, Commander Shaw?'

'I remember,' I said through my teeth.

'But now you are exceeding your brief. That gun. I don't like that. If you'll just lay it on the table . . .'

'Stop fooling, Brennan,' I said. 'It's all up for you. I'm taking you in for questioning.'

'You and who else?'

I said, 'You'll find out.' He wouldn't be knowing I hadn't yet contacted Focal House, but he had every past reason to be aware of what Max and 6D2 HQ Britain could provide at short notice – always provided they got the notice. He could stew now in his uncertainty on that score.

He said conversationally, standing stock-still just inside the doorway, 'It's not a nice night for being out. I only just got through. On foot for a good deal of the way.'

'I can wait,' I said.

He smiled, very much in control of himself. 'And Miss Mandrake? You're aware that your behaviour will rub off on her, I'm sure.'

I didn't respond. What could I have said? I was

aware, all right. I had to step very carefully and I had to remind myself again that I was here on behalf of Pierre Monet and a whole lot of European political considerations. While I remained silent, Brennan spoke again. He said, 'I'm not unaware of events in Bristol.'

'What's that supposed to mean, Brennan?'

'What it says. You didn't imagine I wouldn't be aware, did you?'

'Just tell me,' I said, 'what you were working yourself up to.'

He smiled again. It was just a grimace. 'Percy Excrudd,' he said, not unexpectedly. 'He was released by the police. He went home. There was a police guard. I was unable to speak to him, to find out how much he'd said — *what* he'd said. However little he might or might not have said, there was always the danger that he might say more under pressure.'

'So?'

Brennan shrugged. 'Quite easy. Telescopic sights. Excrudd is dead. A policeman died with him. Also — to be on the safe side — Excrudd's wife.'

There was no point in telling him he was a bastard; he'd always known that for himself. There comes a time with people like Polecat Brennan when you run out of condemnatory words, so I just left it and asked, 'Well? What was it you thought Excrudd might have come up with?'

He shrugged. 'This and that. I'd heard of a visit to his breaker's yard. I fancied you might be involved, Commander Shaw.'

'But you didn't expect to find me here.'

He conceded the point. 'No.'

'Why not?' I asked.

'Because I knew it would be Miss Mandrake you were after before anything else. And Miss Mandrake isn't here. I believed that if Percy Excrudd had given away any addresses, it would be where Miss Mandrake actually is.'

I asked, 'What's behind that sheet of hardboard, Brennan?'

Again the nasty smile. 'Well − not Miss Mandrake, if that's what you're thinking.'

I said abruptly, 'We're going to open it up. Right now.' I gestured with the Biretta. 'Keep your hands away from your sides and lift that hardboard clear. Or better still, we'll have your funny parson lookalike do it.'

Brennan didn't seem worried. He just shrugged, and jerked his head at Fred. 'Do as the man says,' he ordered.

Fred went to the hardboard sheet and lifted it from its retaining runners. Behind, there was a blank space. Just nothing. Fred, holding the hardboard in front of him like a shield, cocked an eyebrow at Brennan. Brennan nodded. Fred reached into the recess, feeling around above his head. He pulled at something. There was a loud click and then a faint hum, something electrical being set in motion. Slowly the back wall began to rise and as it did so, Fred stepped neatly aside, placing himself alongside Brennan and the blowsy woman. I didn't think anything of it. Not then — not in time. When the floor of the kitchen fell away beneath my feet it was too late. Hearing Brennan's mocking laugh, I slid down a steeply angled metal slide, a long way down it seemed, until I hit solid stone slabs at the bottom.

I'd knocked myself out for a while. On hitting the slabs, I believe my head must have jerked back and thwacked against the metal edge of the slide. Anyway, when I came round, presumably not long after, a bare electric light bulb shone, suspended on a short flex from the ceiling. There were handcuffs on my wrists. Brennan was aiming an automatic pistol at my head. Beyond him I saw an open doorway, like the entry to a wine cellar leading off the larger cellar I was in. A house like this would have had a whole network of cellars, all in use in the old days — larder, lamp room, bootroom, coal cellar, that sort of thing, plus the wine cellar. Something told me it didn't contain wine now.

I looked into Brennan's eyes. I asked, 'Now what, Brennan?'

I believed he was going to shoot me. It seemed the obvious thing to do from his point of view. But it seemed that wasn't to happen. Not yet.

Brennan said, 'A little more co-operation, Commander Shaw.'

I gave a rude reply to that.

He said, 'Remember Miss Mandrake.' That was all; and of course I should have known. Felicity was still his trump card.

I said, 'Co-operation looks a likely prospect from here. Doesn't it?'

'Very,' he said coolly. 'I have your transmitter — your handy link with 6D2. I don't think I need say more.'

He didn't; the juxtaposition of that transmitter and the threat hanging over Felicity — it was much too plain. I was going to be forced into passing false information back to Max. And once again the terrible dilemma: where did my first loyalty lie? I knew Max's answer to that well enough. Somehow I had to walk a tightrope, play for time — unless I could get out from under, and that didn't seem a very likely prospect. I cursed myself for not having used that transmitter earlier.

Brennan lost no time in telling me what I had to do.

He said, 'Focal House will be expecting some word from you, Commander Shaw.' He added that he'd checked with his reverend mate that I'd not used the transmitter since my arrival on the scene.

'If they don't get it, they may start looking. Remember Mr Excrudd. I don't want them looking this way. I'm sure you understand.'

I knew what he wanted before he put it into words. I was to give Focal House a bum steer, say I was reaching gold and give Max a false location, somewhere as far as possible from Lower Downham, like the north of Scotland, for instance.

Brennan said, 'I think you get the picture, right? Let's say you've struck lucky in — North Yorkshire?

Somewhere in the cave system around Ingleborough or Horton-in-Ribblesdale. That'll take up a lot of their time.'

'Until next Friday?' I still had the advantage of knowing, which presumably Brennan did not, that the diplomatic exchange of persons French and British had been brought forward by twenty-four hours. That gave me a sort of leeway — until such time as one of Brennan's mob got the word from a mole in high places.

'Until next Friday,' Brennan said in a tone of satisfaction.

He hadn't wanted me to use the transmitter right away. He said the contact would be made while we were on the move — he didn't say where to. I got the idea he didn't want to risk any chance of the transmission itself giving away a locality or direction. I saw one reason — or maybe I should say two reasons — why this should be so when I was pushed ahead of Brennan's automatic, through the wine cellar entry and out by another door opposite. In the wine cellar, on the racks at either side, were the dead bodies of the phoney cleric and his woman companion. They had both been shot through the head, presumably while I'd been unconscious since I hadn't heard any gunfire — and there was a fair amount of blood. They looked immensely pathetic lying there in place of crusted, cobwebbed wine bottles. Two people drawn into something too big for them, no doubt lured by the promise of big money and no more ends of piers or down-at-heel provincial theatres. All they'd got out of it was this: sudden death and lonely decomposition in a wine cellar in snowbound East Anglia. The blood-smeared clerical collar stood out like a rebuke.

I was pushed up a flight of stone steps to the kitchen where the floor was nicely solid again. I was sat awkwardly on an upright chair while Brennan made a pot of coffee and then held a cup to my lips. I wasn't to be left without nourishment. I think it was still dark outside; the curtains remained drawn across the windows. It was desperately cold in the kitchen, but the wind, I believed, had gone or almost gone. The banshee-like sighing and the buffeting around the walls had died away. The snow was going to be there still. Drinking his coffee, Brennan pulled the curtain aside a little way and looked out. He confirmed the lying snow.

For the first time he asked me how I'd got there. I told him the BMW was in a clump of trees down the road towards the village and he nodded.

He'd had to leave his own car behind when the snow got too thick. He'd left it farther back, in the village, outside the church, he said.

I doubted if he was going to suggest using my car; he wouldn't want to leave his around so openly, for one thing. I was proved partly right. And I could see his dilemma: one or other car would have to be left behind and would give away clues. That seemed to be inevitable. But Brennan, of course, had the answer: his own car was one of Percy Excrudd's faked-up registrations and was less likely to be pounced upon than mine when it was found. As for the BMW, he had plans. It was to be destroyed. He would have liked to have dumped it in deep water, but that would have meant a drive to somewhere like Denver Sluice and that, for obvious reasons, was not on.

Because the destruction was best set in train during the night hours, we set off a quarter of an hour later, me still handcuffed in front of Brennan's automatic, and Brennan heaving a two-gallon can of petrol. The BMW made a fantastic bonfire; I was sorry to see it go. With Brennan carrying the number plates, which he had unscrewed prior to the conflagration, we beat it as fast as possible for the church and Brennan's car. There wasn't a soul about as, with some difficulty, Brennan turned the car and drove off over the packed snow for the A10, where he turned left, south towards London.

During the trek from The Moorings to Brennan's car there had been times, in spite of the handcuffs, when I might well have had a chance of making a getaway. I was well enough aware of that. But handcuffed, I could not have made that getaway with a captive Brennan; and obviously I couldn't afford to leave him behind. And overridingly, of course, there was Felicity. I had to stay with Brennan and that was that.

The drive for the A10 had taken some time, going dead slow and coping with a number of skids. Once on the A10 we made better speed – there had been enough traffic to clear tracks through the snow, slushy tracks. Before we reached Ely Brennan stopped the car and fished around for a familiar black bag. This was pulled

101

over my head and I was told to slump forward so that my bagged head wouldn't be too obvious, which it otherwise could be once daylight came. I'd seen from the clock on the dash that the time was 02.35; Brennan had quite a few hours of night driving ahead of him. Some while after this he stopped again and removed the bag. I couldn't make out any landmarks and no road signs, but it looked as though we were on the hard shoulder of a motorway, a motorway with quite a lot of snow on it.

Brennan had my transmitter in his hand.

'This is where you make contact,' he said. 'And I have every reason to believe you won't be saying anything out of turn. Right?'

'As you say.'

'So just listen.' He told me what I was to pass to Focal House. I had followed a lead that had taken me to . . . . 'Not North Yorkshire after all,' Brennan said. 'You wouldn't have had the time.'

'So where?' I asked.

He was having a think, eyes screwed up. After a while he said, 'Southampton. Or let's say Woolston, that's a suburb of Southampton. A house in St Anne's Road. Got that, have you?'

I said I had. Brennan passed over the transmitter and I called Focal House. I gave the address and said I wanted the heavies sent in pronto, initially to stand by. Then I cut the call before any awkward questions could be asked. Brennan was chuckling away to himself, no doubt happy at the thought of the heavy mob speeding down to Southampton Water on a wild-goose chase, arriving to anticlimax and a high degree of bewilderment with no me to meet them and point them precisely in the right direction. I wondered what Max was going to make out of it: there would have been no doubt whatever that it was I who'd made the call, and where was I? When Brennan asked me what I thought they'd do, I said truthfully that really I could make no assessment. He wasn't bothered; it had been just a casual enquiry to add to his pleasure in thinking of the hoo-ha that would be going on in high places.

The call made, the black bag was replaced and Brennan took the car back onto the carriageway. I had no idea in which direction we were heading.

Nor did I, at first, know where we were when things altered rather drastically for both of us.

It was quite a while later, a matter of around three hours I think, and it was still pitch dark, when the bag over my head came off. It was pulled off by a man in an anorak while I lay in the snow on the hard shoulder recovering hazily from a nasty impact. When I was capable of understanding, the man told me he'd been following our car when a lorry had zoomed past in the middle lane and then pulled over dangerously, too soon for Brennan. The lorry had impacted on Brennan's offside front wing and we'd spun. The lorry had gone on its lethal way uncaring, maybe unknowing.

There was something else as well: an abandoned police patrol car and a policeman lying bloodily on the hard shoulder a little way ahead. The policeman was dead, the man said. When the mobile had stopped for a look-see, there had been shots. Brennan, obviously, with his automatic: there was no sign of him now, no more shots after the one burst.

I said, 'You decided to stay. Why?'

'I'm a doctor, that's why. Army medic. We don't run.'

Army medic or not, it was bravery.

I gave the medic an explanation: I was still wearing handcuffs and they looked suspicious, what with the bag and all. My explanation was of necessity unconvincing; the medic said he'd drive me to the nearest police station; that suited me very well, since I needed to get in touch urgently with Focal House. My transmitter had gone with Brennan, as had my Biretta. Before we headed for the police station, where I hoped they'd be able to remove my handcuffs, I asked my Good Samaritan where that nearest nick was.

'Folkestone,' he said.

8

I went from Folkestone to Focal House, by police car. Max had spent the night in the penthouse suite. I guessed he'd be doing that every night until after the visit of the French Foreign Minister.

I gave him a full report. It didn't amount to very much help. He asked about Miss Mandrake. I said I had no information at all except that she was still with them.

'No idea where?'

I shook my head. 'None.'

Max looked very old and tired. Whatever bollockings he had handed out in regard to my personal association with Felicity, I knew he was taking her capture and her continuing ordeal very hard.

He asked, 'Can you make any assessment? I mean in regard to those buggers' plans?'

I said pointedly, 'Brennan made his getaway in Folkestone.'

'Yes. The tunnel?'

'What else?'

Max sighed. 'I've had a number of conversations with the FO.'

'Hedge?'

'Hedge, yes. And the permanent under-secretary, who's rather more with it than Hedge, has talked about the tunnel. The security people absolutely reject the idea of anything going wrong in the tunnel. Apparently they're almost paranoiac about it. Nothing is going to happen in the tunnel. Before or after, yes. That's where they're concentrating their minds.'

'Which,' I said, 'makes the tunnel the more likely. That's if Brennan and his mob suss out the paranoia. And Brennan's no fool — besides which he has his contacts as we know.'

'Yes.' Max threw up his hands in a gesture almost of despair that was, to say the least, uncharacteristic of the Max I'd known for so long. Clearly, the FO had been getting him down. Closed minds, minds that had been assured by the experts that the tunnel was impregnable, that an assassination attempt was most likely to take place in the open. Telescopic sights, as used already on this job by Brennan when he'd shot down Percy Excrudd and his wife and a police officer. Just as I thought about that, Max began to tell me about it.

I said, 'I know. That makes two policemen dead. I'm not so bothered about Percy Excrudd.'

'That setup in, where was it, Lower Downham? I'll have it gone through.' I knew what he meant: fingerprints, forensic, the lot. Those two bodies — I supposed they might yield something; I'd not had the opportunity of looking. But Brennan would have taken care not to leave anything useful behind.

We were absolutely no farther ahead. And once again

Brennan had vanished. Folkestone police, of course, would be out on a murder hunt now, but I reckoned Polecat Brennan could cope with that.

I would be going back down to Folkestone, I told Max. First, he said, I had to have a word with Hedge.

I did, after more cloak-and-dagger stuff.

I was to meet Hedge in the country. In Petersfield, down in Hampshire. In the car park attached to the lake. I was provided with a car by 6D2's transport section. I drove down straight away. Max said Hedge was down there already, another furtive meeting, this time with a retired diplomat living in the vicinity who'd had past experience of assassination attempts and how to deflect them. My visit had been fixed as soon as I'd got through to Focal House from Folkestone and Max had informed the FO that I was back in circulation.

Hedge would be in the car park at noon. We would not make overt contact; such was not the Hedge way. There was a footpath that ran right round the lake; when Hedge had spotted me, he would start walking round the lake in one direction; I would start off the other way, and somewhere around the perimeter we would strike up a conversation.

I reached the car park twenty minutes late; there had been a delay on the A3 near Liphook. At first I didn't recognize Hedge. Gone were the black coat and striped trousers, the bowler and the umbrella. He wore washed-out blue jeans that showed up his pot belly, rather curious footwear and a green Aertex sports shirt under a green anorak. He had an aggrieved air due to his having been kept waiting, and he looked tremendously agitated. I could see he couldn't wait to give me a bollocking for being late.

He waited a while after my arrival in order to deflect suspicion, then he set off round the lake. I duly went the other way. The weather was cold but bright, sunny, with none of the snow that had hit East Anglia. A gentle breeze slightly ruffled the waters of the lake. I walked between trees and bushes, passed two anglers waiting patiently for bites. I reckoned Hedge was not going to like them overmuch: they could be spies, agents of a foreign power waiting either to pounce or to make notes for future use. In point of fact they were obviously harmless, bucolic and preoccupied with fish.

Coming down to the far end of the lake I found Hedge feeding a quacking group of importunate ducks. He had a bag of bread: like any good Foreign Office security man, he'd come prepared.

He caught my eye briefly, then looked away. But I reckoned I'd seen a sort of come-on signal, so I joined him.

'Funny things, ducks,' he said conversationally.

I agreed. 'They'll be hungry in winter. Not so many people to − to cast bread upon the waters.'

He gave me a quick, sideways look. Was I trying to pass something? Biblical quotations could be thus used, I supposed. I was irritated by the whole thing and I decided to tease. Or give him more food for phoney thought. 'Loaves and fishes,' I said. 'By the lake of Gallilee. Wasn't it?'

'Er – '

'Men fishing. Over there.' I pointed the way I'd come.

'Oh.'

'Fishers of men?'

Hedge rustled angrily. 'Really, I don't see – '

'Never mind, it's not important.'

'Not?'

'No.' I wondered how I was going to establish some sort of opening that Hedge might find suitable as an excuse to move on together to a place, if such existed, of greater security. Then an odd and fortunate thing happened. There had been a large black dog, of uncertain but hairy breed, somewhat mangy and very hungry-looking, waiting on the shore for a share of Hedge's largesse. But with no luck: Hedge was concentrating on the ducks in the water. Then the dog had a thought: to be fed you had to be in the water. It flopped in, swam out a short distance, then swam back in and joined the ducks.

'Pretending he's a duck,' I said. We both laughed. Hedge fed bread to the dog.

'Funny things, dogs,' he said. He came to the end of his bag of mouldy bread and, chatting quite naturally about the funniness of dogs and the things they got up to – he'd once known a friend's dog that had been found on a dining-room table after a party, scoffing up a bowl of cream – we moved on, back the way I had come. But within half a minute Hedge stopped and said in a low voice, 'You said men fishing.'

'Yes.'

'We'll go the other way round.'

We turned. I'd been dead right; and Hedge would have already reconnoitred the other way.

We walked along slowly and Hedge asked questions, still using that low voice.

'Lower Downham,' he said.

'Yes?'

'Tell me about it.'

I did so. 'No help,' I said. 'Nothing learned. Two dead bodies, a phoney cleric and a loose-looking woman.'

'Names?'

'Fred.'

'Fred what?'

'No idea. Sorry. Same with the woman.'

Hedge clicked his tongue. 'You don't seem to have achieved much. And I suppose you realize you were late. Really, it's not good enough.' He seethed away for a moment or two. 'And now there's Folkestone. I imagine you're going to suggest the tunnel.'

'Yes,' I said, steering clear of a dog mess between the trees. A little farther on there was another; Hedge put a foot slap in it and swore.

'Bother take it,' he said crossly. He spent a while wiping his shoe on grass and winter-dead leaves. 'Forget it,' he said tersely.

'The dog shit?'

He didn't like the word, I could see that. 'No,' he snapped. 'The *tunnel*!'

'Not so loud, Hedge.'

He hissed at me. 'Oh, for God's sake don't teach me my job and don't use that name! Do use some discretion, *please*. And don't go on about the – you know what. That's a dead issue. The French agree.' He paused, I think importantly. In a lower-than-ever voice he said, 'There's been word from Paris. The embassy, don't you know.'

'Do tell me,' I said, showing interest.

'They have their avenues, you see. A little bird has said the attempt is to be made at Calais. On the shore, you see. On the *French* shore, and thank God for that. If it happens there, we can't be blamed.'

'So the British end's pulling out, is it?'

'Oh, by no means, my dear fellow, no! Little birds – they can be wrong.' You can say that again, I thought to myself; I reckoned that little bird was a bloody liar, and maybe intentionally. Almost certainly intentionally. If there were people like Hedge in the Paris Embassy, it wouldn't be too hard to make them believe anything, I thought.

He went on. The little bird hadn't, it seemed, been terribly explicit. There had been that mention of Calais, or more (or less) exactly somewhere between Paris and Calais. The little bird had suggested a happening on the train but I didn't see this as particularly likely unless they meant to wreck the entire train and Pierre Monet with it, thus perhaps making the thing look not so specifically political. But that, too, was unlikely: I'd gathered that the whole idea was to discommode the EC.

But Hedge was putting a lot of faith in that little bird. He said, 'It's likely to be a German national.'

'The bird?'

'No. The assassin.'

'According to this little bird?'

'Yes.'

'Why?'

'Wheels within wheels,' Hedge whispered conspiratorially. 'You know what these people are like.'

As an answer it was unsatisfactory, but I fancied I understood what he was getting at. Although, of course, on the surface he supported the EC, Hedge was obviously very British underneath − so was I, but in perhaps a more lenient way. Striped pants and bowler hats and a mind that was set in the glorious days of Empire when to be born British was the greatest, most prized gift of God. Foreigners naturally began at Calais and were physically unclean, mentally unsound, as full of tricks as monkeys which in many ways they resembled, never to be trusted, always out for their own ends, oily, ingratiating when it suited them, always at each others' throats. The French ate frogs, the Italians carried knives, the Spaniards were bone idle like the Irish and unsafe with women, the Greeks being different in that respect and prone to buggery, the Germans − well, the Germans. Sauerkraut and short leather trousers, marching songs and militarism, apfelstrudel and unlimited beer. And inimical to Britain. Also inimical, basically, to La France.

Well, yes. If Hedge had actually said all that in addition to (I firmly believed) thinking it, I would have found myself in some measure of agreement. But certainly not all the way. Nevertheless, I saw what he'd been driving at when he'd said You Know What These People Are Like. The Germans would be only too happy to throw the French into some sort of frenzy. Not a difficult thing to do, but I didn't believe they would do it openly.

I said as much.

'I didn't mean to suggest openly,' Hedge said.

'But you said a German assassin — '

'Oh, well, yes, I may have done, but what I meant was the Germans will be *behind* it.'

'So we're back to Polecat Brennan?'

'As the organizer, the backroom boy, yes.'

Of course, Brennan had German collaborators, and French ones as well. Also other nationalities: Ogmanfiller was an American citizen. Brennan was nothing if not cosmopolitan. I decided to ask Hedge the sixty-four thousand dollar question. What, I asked him, was the Foreign Office view?

'On what?'

'On what all the hoo-ha is about? I mean — what's the official view on *why* the French Foreign Minister's to be assassinated? What's in it for who?'

Hedge hedged. He said distantly, 'The Foreign Office prefers not to have views, my dear fellow.'

'Ah, yes. You mean, *officially* it doesn't have views?'

'Exactly.'

'Unofficially, then.'

By this time we had got back to the car park. Hedge slowed his pace; he wasn't going to make another round of the lake because if he went one way he would pass the anglers, and if he went back the way we had come, and then back again to the car park, it would look suspicious. So he spoke on the spot, briefly. He said, 'My dear fellow, it's really rather unprofitable to go into *unofficial* views, isn't it?'

I assumed that meant either the FO hadn't any views at all, or they were simply just as baffled as Max and I were. Hedge went to his car. I went to mine. We drove off, Hedge turning right and apparently heading for the A3 and London, me turning left to head in the general direction of Folkestone. It seemed that the whole meeting had been designed solely to tell me to watch out for a German who would slay the French Foreign Minister before he got to Calais next Thursday. Not even quite that: it wouldn't be a German who actually would do the deed.

Hedge was an ass, and the little bird was a red herring.

And yet, maybe not entirely so. I was still heading down for the coast road that would take me eventually to Folkestone when I was called up on my car radio. Max in person. I was to report to the military police barracks in Chichester. Pronto. That, I knew, meant that orders would be awaiting me, orders that Max wouldn't risk putting out over the air. I had a hunch that the orders might be for Paris. Max had said earlier I'd need to liaise with our Paris HQ. And it wasn't all that far to Gatwick from Chichester.

Pronto, as used by Max, meant all stops were to be pulled out. I put my foot down and was in Chichester twenty minutes later, pulling into the barracks past the guardroom and a redcapped sentry. I was stopped and I made myself known. I was told to park and report to a Major MacAllister, which I did. The orders were not for Paris. They were for Germany. The little bird had maybe got something after all.

A helicopter would await me at the Goodwood aerodrome, not far from where I was. The helicopter would take me to Heathrow where I would take the ordinary schedule for Hanover.

I was accompanied by an MP sergeant as far as the aerodrome and after leaving me he drove the 6D2 car back to the police barracks. I boarded the waiting helicopter and was handed a bulky package. In this I found a new ballpoint transmitter and a new automatic to replace the Biretta removed by Polecat Brennan. There were also a hundred rounds of ammunition. I knew there would be no trouble at Heathrow: Max would have paved the way and in any case the airport security people were well accustomed to the comings and goings of 6D2 agents and they were similarly accustomed at Hanover.

That evening I left the aircraft at Hanover and after

going through the checks I lingered for a cup of coffee in the concourse café. My orders from Max as promulgated in the police barracks were to take a cab to a beer cellar in the town where I would be contacted by an agent I knew, Hans Langer, but he would not be there until 9 p.m. so I had time to fill in.

Idly, I watched the crowds. The rows of shops were still busy with customers. I sat back as anonymously as possible and just observed; often enough there's something to be gained from doing that. In this life of mine, you never knew what might drift past. While I was thus engaged, another incoming aircraft disgorged its passengers. I watched them emerge, watched them being greeted or not being greeted as the case might be.

One who was not greeted was Steenie Ogmanfiller.

She didn't see me. The moment I saw her, I hid my face behind an English-language copy of *The Times* that I'd bought at the bookstall. She went on out and I followed, discreetly.

If necessary, Hans Langer would have to wait.

9

It had been only last night, running into the early hours
of today probably, that Ogmanfiller had been waiting
for me to rendezvous in Piccadilly Underground
station. She must have put her skates on: that incoming
aircraft, if I'd read the arrivals board correctly, had
come from Paris. I wondered what she'd been doing in
Paris.

Maybe I'd be finding out.

She didn't take a taxi. She walked out of the
concourse, no backward looks. She hurried away
somewhere to the right, once outside. Then she broke
into a stumbling sort of run towards a parked car which
got moving almost before she was fully in. So that was
that.

'You didn't get the car's number?' Hans Langer asked.

I had to confess it. 'No. No time − I wasn't very
near.'

Hans nodded through thick-lensed, heavy spectacles.
He was a small man, unprepossessing, rather fat and
with a feather in his Tyrolean-type hat, but he had a
good brain and also he spoke very good English. He

said, 'Anyway, it's interesting that she is here in Germany.'

'Yes. You Germans are not supposed to be involved. I mean the German Government, Hans.'

'Not supposed to be. And in any case Miss Ogmanfiller is not the German Government.'

'Thank the Lord for that. But I didn't suppose she was. I meant, why Ogmanfiller in Germany?'

He shrugged, and took a long pull at his lager. It was Grolsch, and therefore strong, and he'd started with a pint. No doubt the fat absorbed it easily enough. He glanced around – we were in a sort of alcove, thus unlikely to be overheard, but still – then he said, 'Your Mr Hedge.'

'He's not my Mr Hedge and thank the Lord for that as well. But go on.'

'Yes. This Hedge – I have been fully informed, you know – has postulated a German threat from behind the scenes.'

I said, 'Yes, he has. Do you go along with that?'

'Yes. It begins to seem likely.'

'Hence Ogmanfiller? Polecat Brennan's advance party?'

He grinned. 'Not quite that. The execution of the threat . . . this will not of course be in Germany.' Hans paused for a moment, then went on, 'It is *why* Fräulein Ogmanfiller is in Germany that is interesting, as you yourself have suggested. I suggest an answer to the *why*. She is here merely to meet someone.' He sighed and drank more Grolsch, belching a little as he did so. 'It is much of a pity that you lost her, Commander.'

'Right,' I said, 'but don't rub it in. Let's hope she can be picked up again.'

'We shall try.' His eyes gleamed behind the thick lenses. 'We know some facts about Fräulein Ogmanfiller that it is possible you do not know – '

'Recently acquired?'

'In some instances, yes. You must already know that Ogmanfiller . . . . the family came originally from Germany, from the days of Hitler, the early days, the burning of the Reichstag and so on. The grandparents Ogmanfiller left Germany for America.'

I told him yes, we knew all that. What, I asked, was fresh?

'There are relatives still in Germany. Not by the name of Ogmanfiller. Distant relatives by marriage – there was some difficulty with Goebbels on account of the marriage to a Jewish family, but they nevertheless became Party members before the 1939 war. The family name was – and is – a common one, Schmidt.' Hans paused again. His tankard was empty: I signalled a waiter and ordered more. For Hans, not for me: I felt I was going to need a clear head, and not having had much sleep except on the jet from Heathrow, I was dead tired. The ambience of the beer cellar, the low lights, the laughter and the crowd, all were tending to lull me almost to sleep and that wouldn't do at all.

Hans went on, 'Heinrich Schmidt is the one that interests us. Heinrich Schmidt is a distant cousin of our Ogmanfiller. Heinrich Schmidt is a neo-Nazi and is among the most extreme of them.' Another pause. 'This Schmidt — he lives in a town about an hour's drive south of Hanover. In Rinteln. It is possible, I think, that that is why Ogmanfiller has come here to Germany. To make contact with Heinrich Schmidt.'

I nodded. I agreed it was possible. Rinteln might be worth a visit. It occurred to me that Felicity might have been smuggled into Germany — that would be difficult, but far from impossible. There would be ways open to Polecat Brennan and his confederates; most likely by sea — a coaster leaving a British port, bound, say, for Hamburg or Wilhelmshaven but making an unauthorized call en route, maybe lying offshore, and a boat coming out, all under cover of a dark night . . . .

I wasn't going to speak of Felicity just then. I didn't want Hans to get the idea that personal considerations took priority. I went back instead to what he'd said earlier. I said, 'Hans, you indicated that the German Government was not *supposed* to be involved in the big threat. What exactly did you mean by that?'

He didn't answer right away. While he was not answering, the waiter came with the order and he sank his face in the tankard. Froth dangled from the end of his nose. He wiped it away. He began then to answer my question. He said, 'There is a clandestine involvement on the part of some members of the government, those with Nazi sympathies that they are not intended to have. These persons wish — '

I didn't get to hear which persons wished what. Hans broke off as a commotion started up just inside the entry to the beer cellar. There were shouts, yells, cries of what seemed to be pain. Down the steps came a surge of young people, men and women, the men in jackboots, all of them with Nazi slogans and swastikas on their clothing, clothing that appeared to be a uniform, and they carried banners again showing the swastika superimposed on the old, prewar Nazi flag. As they came down, fighting broke out all over. Tables were overturned and smashed, chairs were lifted as clubs to break heads. I saw the dull gleam of gunmetal in the cellar lights just before they went out.

Now there was bedlam.

I felt Hans's hand on my arm. 'We get out now,' he said in a high voice, 'if we can. Keep close.'

'Shoulder to shoulder,' I said.

We moved away from our alcove and tried to push through in the direction of the exit. Bodies were everywhere and I slithered in a patch of what I believe was blood. The noise was indescribable. I was pushing, shoving, hitting out whenever I was obstructed, not bothered whether it was a Nazi or a non-Nazi. To get out was all; I couldn't risk being arrested by the German police who would be along at any moment, I couldn't risk becoming involved in Germany's internal politics, couldn't risk not being believed until it was too late.

Hans was clinging onto me: I could sense his enormous fear. I took a blow on the head, a glancing blow from something that felt like a gun barrel, and momentarily I staggered, almost lost my balance but was brought up short by what I think was a female breast, a really big and cushiony one. I carried on pushing through for the exit, managing not to part company with my overnight bag. At last I made it. Hans was still with me. As we came out into the street we heard, still distant, the sound of police sirens. When we were some way from the beer cellar the police vehicles came in. Cops poured out of them. We ran like greased lightning. Then the police opened fire. They were very accurate: I heard the half-stifled gasp from Hans, was aware of the little fat man falling to the ground just behind me. There was no more firing, at least not in our direction; the police were now in battle with the mob, the Nazis and non-Nazis pouring out from the beer cellar, fighting mad still.

There was an alley just to our left, and I dragged Hans into it. There was blood spreading through his clothing from his stomach. His eyes beseeched me; he was trying to say something, perhaps to finish his answer to my question. He never made it; he gave a final gasp, more blood surged, blood and foam appeared on his lips. A jerk of his body and that was the end. Hans died there in that alley, a dirty alley with dog faeces and general rubbish. There was nothing I could do other than vanish. I ran along the alley, away from the police direction. The alley was a fairly short one; I came out into a small, neat square, very clean, with tall old buildings that reminded me of illustrations in a book about the Pied Piper of Hamelin. I moved on, crossing the little square, putting more distance between me and the disturbance around the beer cellar. I could still hear the racket.

I wondered what to do next.

6D2 had no presence in Hanover: Hans Langer had come from the Berlin HQ − we'd shifted from Bonn after the reunification of Germany. Berlin was quite a distance; but I had come to Germany for a purpose, Max's purpose, even if I didn't yet know what it was. And Hans Langer, who would have told me, who was I believed on the point of telling me, was dead in that alley. And something was telling me that Rinteln was not only much closer than Berlin but also Ogmanfiller or her relative might be a better prospect in the circumstances as they had turned out.

Heinrich Schmidt was the name. Heinrich Schmidt, neo-Nazi whose ambition, probably, was to reincarnate the memory and the times of Adolf Hitler, Chancellor of the Third Reich, the Reich that was to have lasted a thousand years.

Heinrich Schmidt might well be seeing Ogmanfiller as a means to an end. Assassinations had throughout history changed rulers and policies, boundaries and dynasties and power blocs. The new Nazism would stand little chance under a European federation.

I decided to go to Rinteln. From there I could contact Berlin. So I could from here in Hanover, but I didn't want to approach the local police with a request to be put in touch by use of their security telephone. Not tonight. Also, I didn't want to be perhaps deflected from Rinteln by order of Berlin. Once I was there I was there, a *fait accompli*. Once again I was becoming personal. Time was running out and I had to get my hands on Felicity before it was too late.

I hitched a lift.

Following the signposts, I started walking along the road to Rinteln, soon coming to an autobahn. I stuck out my thumb and after a while a lorry stopped. The driver was English, the lorry, a heavy artic, was from Sheffield by way of Hamburg, and it was heading down to Hamelin via Minden and Rinteln itself which was a piece of luck. I heaved my overnight bag in.

I chatted with the driver. I spun him a yarn that my car had broken down in Hanover and I had to get back to Rinteln that night. A sick wife, I said.

'Sorry to hear that, mate. But it's maybe my lucky day.'

'Oh? How's that?'

'My first visit to Rinteln. I have to find the hospital. Know where it is, do you?'

As it happened, I did. I'd been in Rinteln a number of years before, when the British Army of the Rhine had been at full strength. The hospital, a Nazi military hospital during the war, built in the shape of a swastika, was then a British one. I didn't know what it might be now; the end of the Soviet Union had wrought many changes to the West's defensive structure and now there was not much of a British military presence. Anyway, I was able to give the driver general directions. I wouldn't be with him when I got there because he had a load to drop in Minden and wouldn't be going on until the morning, which meant I would have to make my own arrangements for my onward transport.

The driver went on talking: he was the talkative sort and he liked the companionship. He was, he said, carrying a cargo of machine parts for Minden, Rinteln and Hamelin. They were all consigned to the one firm even though the deliveries were for the three factories.

'And the hospital?'

'Just a part load. I'll get directions there. For the factory like.' He paused, eased himself in his seat. 'Unless you happen to know, mate?'

I sensed difficulty on that one. I said, 'Well, I don't know. I – me and my wife – we're only there on holiday.' Then, in order to sound helpful, I asked, 'What's the name of this factory, what's the firm?'

He pointed to some documents on the shelf in front of me. 'All there, mate,' he said.

I gave the documents a casual glance. Then I saw the name. Defflinger-Zwickau. And the addresses for delivery.

My mind somersaulted back to London. To the tube journey with Hedge that had terminated at Wood Green. Hedge had been hissing information at me at the moment that the hippie had trod on his foot and had advised him to keep his fuckin' feet from under. The information had been nothing more, in fact, than the passing of two names, two names of persons known to be Nazi or Fascist extremists. One was French: the only known name, Louis X. The other German: Gerhardt von Defflinger-Zwickau. Hedge's department had dug up the information that these two had a connection, a positive one according to Hedge, with Polecat Brennan. And both were rabidly against the concept of Federal Europe.

Rinteln beckoned ever more strongly.

I believed I was on the right track. Or anyway, a track that had potential.

I reached Rinteln in the early hours. It was a sleepy old town anyway, and at that hour there was no one around at all. In Minden, after disembarking from the artic, I'd nicked a bicycle. That had helped. I left the bicycle just beyond the hospital, walked on still laden with my overnight bag, crossed a bridge over the River Weser, walked past a riverside catering establishment that might do for breakfast later on, and entered the town. The Defflinger-Zwickau building was in fact on the other side of the town and a little way into the country; I had established this fact from a large sign, an advert really, just before the bridge. That sign had given precise directions but I wasn't yet ready to follow them – was, in fact, doubtful if I would. I could stand out a mile and a visit would be unlikely to produce any sort of helpful result. Not unless I could pick up Ogmanfiller making her way there for a confab or something, and that would be a long shot. She would be unlikely to conduct her business on the Defflinger-Zwickau premises. More likely in the home of her relative by marriage, Heinrich Schmidt.

Frustration loomed. It was a case of so near and yet

so far. In the meantime I didn't want to draw attention to myself if anyone should happen to be peering out of a window and wonder why I was wandering aimlessly around in the night — a very cold one, incidentally, with a light snow beginning to fall now — so I looked around for shelter. There wasn't much; but after a while I found a church and it wasn't locked. So I went in and lay down on a pew at the back. It was a cold place with an unfriendly feel about it, grim and hard. There was a light burning over an altar and in this rather dim light all I could see were dark stone walls, featureless, no memorials, nothing at all. It wasn't quite your friendly country church with a lived-in feel and family histories there for the reading to pass a lonely night. However being more dead tired than ever, I fell asleep.

I suffered nightmares in that hard, unyielding pew. I saw Max tearing his hair in Focal House, yelling abuse at me for having got nowhere. I saw clocks and calendars ticking away towards the end. I saw Hedge removing his fuckin' feet from the hippie, saw him circling the lake at Petersfield and being caught by one of the anglers' lines and dragged beneath the water, crying out to me to help him but not to be seen doing so in case the anglers were spies.

I saw Felicity in Polecat Brennan's grasp and I saw the whip . . .

When, blearily, I woke, my watch showed the time as a little after eight thirty. I got up, lurched unseen, so far as I knew, out of the church and headed back towards the River Weser and that café. I had breakfast, egg and German sausage and coffee, then a wash in the lavatory and felt a good deal better. That done, I found the local police HQ and made myself known. Even in Rinteln they were aware of the international reputation of 6D2 and they didn't poke their noses into the whys and wherefores of my business. They gave me a line to Berlin. I reported the death of Hans Langer and I told them where I was and that I intended remaining in Rinteln, anyway for the time being. I said I was not far off the nub of events; they reminded me of the passing time. I said I was well aware of that, thank you. They asked me what I intended to do.

'No idea,' I said, and that was very nearly the simple truth. 'Has there been anything new from London?' I asked.

'Nothing.'

'Paris?'

Likewise nothing. I asked if there had been any change of plan, and they told me there had not. Obstinacy was much in the air. Stiff-necked French, shades of General de Gaulle. Stiff-necked British too — Churchill and Lady Thatcher. I considered it sheer stupidity.

Four days to go. Just four days. And no one in government had got anywhere *vis-à-vis* the threat. Neither had I, anyway to the extent that I was no nearer putting a stranglehold on Polecat Brennan and his schemes.

But it wasn't all blackness and doom. Not yet. I was

still convinced that I was close to the heart of the thing. The proximity of Ogmanfiller, the Defflinger-Zwickau name, the Nazi connection as evidenced by Heinrich Schmidt, little Hitler-to-be? Or perhaps the new Führer was to be Gerhardt von Defflinger-Zwickau with Heinrich Schmidt as his Göring. For that was the way I began to see this thing developing. And Ogmanfiller? She might make a Goebbels, except that she was only in this for the money. Brennan and Ogmanfiller were obviously due for a massive pay-off.

It was when I'd left police HQ that I began to see the way clear. I was doing no good, hanging about on the periphery. I had to get close, I had to get into the centre. I had to learn exactly what was going on. And after that I had to find a way of getting Felicity out from under and alerting London to the facts. And that, of course, would be the hard part, the part that might never come about.

But I knew I had to take the risk.

The first part would be easy enough: I had to turn myself into the target. Ogmanfiller and Schmidt would be needles in a haystack. But I would not.

I walked around openly; but not too openly. That might not look in character. So I managed to look somewhat furtive, looks cast over my shoulder, that sort of thing, a kind of lurking in shadows. I sat in another café, smoking and half hiding behind a newspaper, a German one. I read through it with genuine interest. There was quite a coverage of the forthcoming exchange of Foreign Ministers via the tunnel, about how the visits would cement the European Community, a lot of blah about friendship and shared interests, a rejection of all the old enmities that had existed for centuries between Britain, Germany and France, right back to William the Conqueror and beyond. All in the past now. The Eurotunnel was the last great symbol. Never mind that it had been in operation for quite a few months now and all this had been spouted at the time of the official opening, the fact of Pierre Monet and Humphrey Chatterton crossing in the tunnel had the press in a bath of sanctimonious bullshit. Yet underneath it I detected something different. Chagrin that Germany itself was not taking part in the exchange visits? Or a basic antagonism starting to emerge against both the British and the French? It was hard to say; but I believed it was there. To Germans, the Fatherland concept would never be submerged.

People came and went in that café. No Ogmanfiller – that would have been too much to hope for. I reserved my decision made on my early-morning arrival in Rinteln: I would go out to the Defflinger-Zwickau complex after all. I would go, not furtively but as myself, making enquiries. The local bosses of Defflinger-Zwickau wouldn't be aware of the information passed to me by Hedge, but the fact that someone from Britain was snooping around would be very quickly reported to Ogmanfiller or Heinrich Schmidt. That was, if my hypothesis was correct.

I took a taxi out to the complex. I didn't fancy the walk in the snow, which was deepening.

* * *

I would go in as an official from Brussels, a British inspector from the European Commission. I would even quote Sir Leon Brittan himself. An inspector of what? Not of political views; not of Nazi connections. There were a number of possibilities: weights and measures came to mind, sanitary matters, hours of employment, accounts, stores, records. Something in the first instance to get past the security guard that I knew would be on the gate. After that, events would themselves take charge, take me – I was convinced of this – where I planned to go. So I settled on stores.

Not that it mattered as things turned out.

The taxi stopped at the gate and I delivered my spiel to the custodian, a middle-aged man wearing some kind of uniform, like Securicor. Naturally enough, I was unable to produce any authorization from the Commission but I showed the man my 6D2 pass. I don't believe he knew what it was but it looked nicely official and he seemed satisfied. He passed directions and waved the taxi through and we were some hundred or so metres inside the gate when I saw Steenie Ogmanfiller.

She saw me too. I was aware of being recognized. I saw the reaction in her face as she glared through the window – she, too, was in a car, though not a taxi. It had the look of a firm's staff car. I saw her speak to the man sitting by her side. The car put on speed. I looked round through the rear window. The Ogmanfiller car had stopped at the gate and the barrier was going down. I let the taxi driver take me to the grand entry to the reception area. I got out and paid him and he drove back towards the gate in the swirling snow.

I went into the reception hall, and I waited. Within a couple of minutes Ogmanfiller loomed, with escort. I didn't like the look of the escort, who was thuggish and had his right hand deep in the pocket of his double-breasted suit. I knew the stance. But things were working out the way I'd planned.

Steenie Ogmanfiller came angularly up to me, smiling like a snake might smile at its victim before striking. Her acne shone, touched up by the snow.

'Well now,' she said nasally. 'Just fancy, finding an old friend right here.'

'A pleasure indeed,' I said. 'And how's Polecat Brennan keeping?'

'You'll be able to ask him that in person,' she said, still smiling. 'Care to come for a ride, would you?'

'That's very civil of you,' I said.

The smile, or anyway the lips, widened and a hiss came out. 'Just don't try anything we wouldn't like,' she said. Her escort moved casually behind me, close, and I felt what I'd known was in his hand. Gunmetal. I was urged towards the door. No one had noticed anything: just old friends meeting unexpectedly. Out of the door, down the steps into the snow, and into the staff car. I went into the back with the escort, whom I thought was probably Heinrich Schmidt. Ogmanfiller sat in front with the driver. We drove out through the gates, past the now lifted barrier, and Ogmanfiller spoke again.

She said, 'Dirty double-crosser,' turning in her seat to stare at me.

I raised an eyebrow. 'You mean Piccadilly Underground?' I asked. I added solicitously, 'I hope you didn't have too long and lonely a wait. I suppose you could have been taken for a lady of easy virtue — if it hadn't been for the acne.'

'You'll pay for that,' she said viciously. 'I'm really going to enjoy this. I really am.'

I didn't doubt it; and for Felicity's sake I much regretted my unkind remark about the acne.

10

This time, no black bags: I was able to see where we were going. Back into the town, or anyway the outskirts, not very far. The trip ended in a debris-strewn yard, not unlike the Percy Excrudd premises in distant Bristol. A yard, and a warehouse with big double doors. The driver got out to open these doors and then we drove in and they were shut behind us. I saw in the dim light straggling through barred windows that the warehouse was stacked with crates. Heavy, unmarked crates. No use my asking what was in them. There would be no answers. I did chance one question.

I asked, 'Are you holding Miss Mandrake here?'

Ogmanfiller said, 'No comment.' That, of course, might have meant anything. As for Polecat Brennan, Ogmanfiller had already hinted I'd be meeting him soon, but I didn't see him emerging from behind those crates.

I was pushed ahead of the thug's gun, right through the warehouse and out into the open and the snow by way of another door. Now we were in a kind of courtyard, a biggish space fringed by buildings, offices and more warehouses. There was no sign of any workforce and there didn't seem to be any lights anywhere though the day was dark with the snowclouds. We went into the office block, into a room furnished with a big desk, a filing cabinet and a number of hard, upright chairs ranged along one of the walls. There was just one window, small, and barred like those in the warehouse.

I was told to sit on one of the chairs. I did so. Under the cover of the thug's gun, Ogmanfiller tied me securely to that chair, using a length of thin but immensely strong rope that she had brought from a drawer in the desk. That done, Ogmanfiller sat in a swivel chair behind the desk and the thug stood by the door with his gun ready for action.

Ogmanfiller said 'Right, Commander Shaw. Now the interrogation.'

'About what?' I asked innocently.

'You don't need to ask. Just answer. If you don't, the guy gets nasty.'

I looked across at the guy. He looked nasty already. I turned to Ogmanfiller. 'Go ahead,' I said easily. 'Not that I've anything to say.'

'You'd better have,' she said. 'First thing: how come you turned up in Rinteln?'

I tried to shrug, but the ropes prevented me. That rope was already biting into my flesh, hard. I said, 'It just happened. You won't believe that, of course.'

'Dead right,' she said in a harsh voice. 'You knew something and I want to know what that something is. Right?'

I didn't answer. She glanced at the thug; he took the hint, and moved towards me. Slowly, keeping his gaze on my face, he fumbled in his pocket and brought out a pack of cigarettes. He lit one, using a Rowenta lighter. I knew what was coming next and I was right. The thug drew deeply on the cigarette, then placed the end on my left earlobe. I felt acute pain and smelled burning flesh. The cigarette was removed and Ogmanfiller, smiling, asked, 'Well, Commander Shaw?'

I said I had nothing to say. The pantomime was repeated on my other ear. I knew this was just for starters. It was. More questions were asked: what was known in London and Paris about the threat, what were the countermeasures, were the governmental plans for the big meeting being altered, and if so, in what way?

I said I knew nothing; I'd been out of contact, in the field, divorced from base. I didn't expect Ogmanfiller to believe that either and she didn't. She retaliated; or rather the thug did. They had plenty of imagination. Small, very thin candles with steel tips were brought from another drawer in the desk and were inserted beneath my fingernails and the candles were lit. I was told the pain would become immense. It already was.

I set my teeth and didn't answer the questions. I kept thinking about Felicity. I thought also that I could perhaps confuse the issue for them by succumbing to pain and talking. Giving false answers. But I knew that wouldn't work. When they found out they'd been double-crossed, it would be Felicity who would suffer as well as me.

Having Felicity, they had the lot. They had the stranglehold drawn tight.

The pain increased. They tried other things, very imaginative, very refined. By this time Ogmanfiller was in a filthy mood. She got up and came over to me. I smelled sweat. She lifted a hand and struck me viciously across the face a number of times, alternately using the back and front of her hand. Heavy rings tore my cheeks. She said, 'Okay, then. We dump him, Heinrich.'

Heinrich. Heinrich Schmidt. I hadn't been wrong. For what good the knowledge would do me now. I didn't like the implications of being dumped.

Out of the office block, back into the courtyard. Into one of the other buildings. Naked now, and naturally without my gun and my replacement pencil transmitter. It was bitingly cold in the courtyard, all that falling snow, and only infinitesimally warmer inside that next building, icy cold again when we came out the other side into a small yard. In the centre of the yard was a well. A real old-timer, an antique complete with handle and rope and lid. Ogmanfiller removed the lid and shone a torch down. I saw the reflection when I was made to bend over the rim and look down. The reflection from the water surface, or was it a mirror? I believed it was a mirror − I'd seen something similar in a pub in Devon, in Fenny Bridges. Very realistic. So was this: Ogmanfiller confirmed that it was a mirror.

'Two-way,' she said. 'You'll be able to look up through it.'

Which I assumed meant I was going down into the well for safe keeping. I hoped it was warmer than up here. Safe keeping could mean refrigeration: I was still naked. And still tied, if not to the chair.

Ogmanfiller dumped the lid beside the well and pulled out one of the bricks that helped to form the wellhead. She fiddled about inside, there was a faint hum, and the mirror began to tilt. When it was up-and-down, it stopped. Under it, I saw metal treads cemented into the side of the well. No water, which was something.

'Down the well,' Ogmanfiller said. Heinrich Schmidt advanced closer with his gun. The barrel jarred against my spine. I said, 'Just tell me how I get down. Or are you going to untie me?'

They didn't untie me. I was told to climb up on the edge of the wellhead, which I did, and then the lowering rope was attached around my waist, and with Heinrich taking the strain on the handle I was given a sudden push that sent me over the edge to clang against the mirror and the lowering began. Bumping from side to side in the descent, I reached bottom. The slack of the rope was chucked down after me. Up top there was a dull thud as the mirror slotted back into place.

Then there was silence.

I don't know how long that silence lasted, but it was broken by a sort of strangled whistling sound and, eerily, I heard the Ogmanfiller voice.

'You'll stay right there till you decide to talk, Commander Shaw. I'll be in touch — this is a two-way communication and what you say will be picked up. So it's up to you, okay?' There was a click, maybe a kind of over-to-you.

I said, 'Okay.' I couldn't make out where the voice was coming from and since it was pitch dark in that well I couldn't see any gadgetry. A moment later the voice came up again.

'See here,' Ogmanfiller said. 'Food for thought, right? You don't talk, you're no goddamn use to us, may as well be dead. In which case, you could get left down there for ever while we go into action. Just think about it, right?'

That was all.

Ogmanfiller had a point.

I did think about it, rather hard. I was caught all ends up, virtually a dead duck. There would be no way out. Around that well would be solid earth, miles and miles of it, so the removal of loose brickwork, if there was any, would be a waste of time. Yet I didn't believe they would kill me. Not yet – not yet.

I had no means of assessing time, which dragged.

I'd taken stock of my situation. For what that was worth.

Obviously there was no way out.

After I'd been, like pussy, down the well for what seemed half a lifetime there was a small click and the Ogmanfiller voice came through.

'Well?' she asked.

I gave a hollow laugh. 'An appropriate comment,' I said.

'Glad you find it funny. That feeling won't last, believe me. Anything to talk about, have you?'

'Nothing relevant,' I said.

'Think of your Miss Mandrake.'

'I am.'

'Then you're a shit,' Ogmanfiller said, and that was all. The intercom clicked off. I knew what she'd said was right; but I still had my other loyalties. I had to do what I could, which currently was nil, for Max and Pierre Monet and for the European Community which didn't seem to be doing very much for Britain. I recalled what Ogmanfiller had said earlier: I might simply be left to rot, left for ever down in that well, a damp and slimy place. Obviously disused for a very long time, but still damp from some previous existence. Odd living creatures scurried — I don't know what they were but guessed from the creepy-crawly feel on my skin that they were spiders, though I didn't see what they could find to live on down there.

I visualized Ogmanfiller and Uncle Heinrich, or whatever the relationship might be — third-cousin-thrice-removed Heinrich? — waiting anxiously for me to say something helpful, waiting for me to crack. I had to fight down a feeling that to crack would be a very wise thing to do, a nice, safe thing. I felt it even more when a good deal later, or so it seemed, Ogmanfiller came on the foetid air with something else.

Using her intercom she said, 'You have five more minutes, Commander Shaw.'

I said, 'Oh, yes. And then what?'

I heard her laugh, heard her saying something I didn't catch, presumably to Heinrich Schmidt. Then she said, 'There is a flooding valve. Connected to the mains water supply. Get it, do you?'

I got it all right. There I was, helpless at the bottom of the well, arms tied. The situation I was in was directly comparable to that of the old wartime shell-handling parties aboard the battleships and cruisers of the day. When a ship went to action stations the handling parties were down at the bottom of deep steel-lined shafts, with the watertight doors clipped down hard at the top of the shaft, clips that could be opened up only from outside. When action came, and if the ship was hit by enemy shells in such a position that the captain on the bridge decided that any one of the magazines was in danger of blowing up, then the order would be passed to flood; and the flooding valves in the shafts would be opened, and seawater would enter. The trapped ratings would be lifted on the rising water until they impinged on the clipped-down hatch, and there they would drown, for the watertight covers would not be lifted with the ship in danger.

That, now, was me. Or soon would be, if Ogmanfiller kept her threat.

She did. When the given time was up, I heard the sudden hiss of water coming down from overhead, from a valve that must have been below the mirror. It came down fast; I was drenched within a matter of seconds. Soon the water was ankle deep, and rising fast. By the time it had reached my shoulders I was well and truly afloat. Ogmanfiller had said earlier that I would be able to see through the mirror, but I couldn't since there was no light on the other side.

But I felt it. I felt it when I rose to the top and my head impacted on it. This had to be the end. The intercom gadget was now below the waterline; it had to be. The voice sounds had not come from above my head. Had it been handy and usable, I just don't know what I would have done. As it was, I suffered what I'd always heard was suffered by drowning persons: a recap of my life. Or anyway, at this pre-drowning state, some of it. Felicity — principally Felicity; Max, in the lush comfort of his suite in Focal House, doing his nut because I wasn't achieving any results; and Hedge of the Foreign Office, dreaming up some stupid, roundabout rendezvous in unlikely places.

Then the first helpless mouthful of water, heralding eventually soaked and bloated lungs. The the insurge stopped: just in time.

I was in fact half-drowned when the mirror was tilted and hands reached down and grabbed hold of me. Hauled out to lie on the ground, I was given the kiss of life by Heinrich Schmidt. A heavy weight pressed down again and again on my chest and I acted as a kind of human waterspout. Dimly I saw Polecat Brennan looking down at me. He looked anxious, and bloody angry too. Ogmanfiller was there, wearing a chastened look. I gathered later, when I'd recovered, that Brennan had turned up unexpectedly and had been livid, to say the least, when Ogmanfiller had reported on where I was. Ogmanfiller had exceeded her authority, gone too close to the brink, too great a risk in the interest of getting me to talk, expecting a pat on the back if she'd succeeded in making me talk. Uncle Heinrich had come in for a tongue-lashing as well.

When I was more or less free of water I was given a shot of brandy, I was warmed before an electric fire and I was wrapped in a heavy blanket with the texture of a horse blanket. Later I was given clothes. A pair of coarse trousers, a belted tweed jacket, shirt, underwear, heavy brown boots. I felt Germanic. All this time, no questions. A nasty, foreboding silence was broken only when I asked about Felicity.

'She's okay,' Brennan said briefly. 'For now.'

That was all. Situation unchanged, except that I was still heady with the reality of being alive after all. I asked again where Felicity was but again I didn't get an answer. What I did get was a propagandic sight of the guns held by Brennan, Schmidt and Ogmanfiller, and then felt more rope securing my wrists behind my back and another length round my upper arms, just to be on the safe side.

Then I got something else: an exposition. Brennan came up, unexpectedly and very briefly, with what he proposed to do. And from the very fact of his coming clean as it were, I knew that my number was up just as surely as if I'd been left in the well to drown.

What Brennan came up with made a kind of mad sense. It was possible of execution, given Polecat

Brennan's widespread net of intrigue and operatives, his proven ability to infiltrate the tightest of organizations, his access to much money through his alliances with terrorist outfits all over the world: Libya, Iraq, Italy, Germany, France, Algeria. In outline it was simple, and there was to be no bomb.

'No bomb?' I said in mock surprise: the assassin's bullet was a much more likely thing. Brennan read my mind, smiling nastily.

'No bullet either,' he said.

'But a tunnel. *The* tunnel?'

'Yes, certainly the tunnel,' he said.

I asked how he meant to go about that. I didn't see the tunnel turning into an assassin of its own volition. Not without assistance.

Brennan said, 'First you must understand, as I do, how the tunnel operates. Do you understand this?'

'Vaguely,' I said. 'I'm willing to learn.'

He nodded. 'Good. Now, the trains go through very fast, as no doubt you know — '

'Two hundred and fifty kph,' I said.

'Yes. Six hundred trains a day — three hundred in each direction. This requires very careful time-keeping, very careful control. The two running tunnels each contain a single track, and each is of 7.6 metres diameter. Not very much space on either side of the very fast-running train.' Brennan paused. 'Any mishap in the tunnel while a train is going through would lead to a total shatter of coachwork, track and persons.'

'So you intend a mishap, Brennan?'

'Yes.'

'Or two mishaps?'

He looked puzzled. 'Why two, Commander Shaw?'

I shrugged. 'Okay, then. You're not intending to involve the British Foreign Secretary in this. Only Pierre Monet. Otherwise you'd need two mishaps, wouldn't you? One in each tunnel?'

Brennan smiled. 'You don't fully understand the tunnel,' he said. 'You haven't studied its construction, its *modus operandi*, perhaps. I, on the other hand, have.'

I made no comment. I was unsure whether or not Brennan might be trying to pick my brains, get me to let something slip that would help him out in a spot where perhaps his own knowledge was not quite so complete as he was making out. Could be; but if he was, then he was under a misapprehension: I genuinely didn't know the detailed work-out. My visit to the tunnel exhibition hadn't revealed the operating techniques. If I'd had more time the last few days, guessing as I had that the Eurotunnel was in some way involved and never mind the snooty pooh-poohing from Hedge and the FO, then I would have made a point of learning what I could. But I hadn't, so that was that.

And a moment later I knew that Brennan wasn't seeking info from me. He really did know it all.

He said, 'The tunnel has crossover points. The tunnels are fifty kilometres long and each are divided into three sections by these crossover points. Two of them, one on the English side, one on the French. This is for emergency use and for maintenance, which takes place at night. In between the two running tunnels there is a service tunnel, linked by cross-passages to each of the running tunnels.'

'So?'

Brennan said, 'If the shuttle carrying Pierre Monet from Calais and Humphrey Chatterton from Folkestone — if one of these shuttles is crossed over into the path of the other, there will be a very spectacular crash.'

I stared back at Polecat Brennan. The crash, the terrible impact of trains meeting each other head on at immensely high speeds would indeed be spectacular, though hidden from sight deep below the waters of the English Channel. The slaughter in those confined tunnels would be horrifying, not to be thought of. Yet it was probably going to happen. Polecat Brennan would see it through. He had never been the man to make empty threats, and the whole of this thing was directed towards the death of Pierre Monet. Brennan would never draw back on humanitarian grounds, would reject as irrelevant any moral consideration that in order to bring about the death of one man, or perhaps two, hundreds of innocent men, women and children would have to die.

The question uppermost in my mind was: *why*?

11

Brennan went on with his exposition. To cross the shuttles over from one tunnel to the other could not be done from outside as it were. He needed to penetrate the system. The heart, lungs and liver of the system were in the control setups at Folkestone and Calais. A very security-guarded and secret place, no visitors other than the odd VIP. From here, among other security arrangements, the television screens would, hour in hour out, 365 days a year, watch the progress or otherwise of every shuttle that passed along the tunnels in each direction. The moment anything untoward happened, it would be known in Folkestone and in Calais.

'By which time it'll be too late,' Brennan said. 'All they will be able to do will be to sort out the mess.'

'And what about getting the trains to cross?'

'That is taken care of,' Brennan said.

'You already have your people on the inside?'

He nodded. 'In the control centre, yes. For some considerable time past. We've always believed we might one day have a use — and now everything is ready.' He paused; I didn't like the way he was looking at me. I was soon apprised of the reason for the look, which was a superior and gloating one. 'For Thursday, Commander Shaw.'

'Thursday,' I repeated rather stupidly. It had shaken me: he wasn't supposed to know, but it seemed he did. He went on to confirm this. He spoke of moles, those useful animals. I felt sick. The EC's last hope had gone, I thought. As had mine; under the surface I'd been banking on Brennan being wrong-footed on the date.

'Three days from now,' he said, rubbing it in.

I didn't comment. I believe he was unaware that I, too, had known of the date change. I thrust down the sick feeling and asked my burning question, 'What's it really in aid of, Brennan? Just why – *why* is it so essential to assassinate Pierre Monet?'

Brennan looked across at Heinrich Schmidt. Something passed between them, a meaningful look. It was Schmidt who answered my question. He said in heavily accented English. 'We of the extreme Right . . .'

'In Germany?'

'In Germany, yes. We believe in the old ideals of our long-dead Führer, he who wished always for the supremacy of the Fatherland, he who would never have joined any such community as is now established in Europe – never would the Führer have submitted his will to that of France, or England, or any other country. The Führer intended the Third Reich to last a thousand years, to be a great world power in its own right, dependent only upon its German citizenry, all pure

Aryans, fine and stalwart sons and daughters of the Reich, faithful to their beloved Führer . . .'

I cut in, stemming the flow of bullshit. 'So this is simply a way of putting a spanner in the works of the European Community?'

'Yes.'

'A *German* spanner? Specifically German?'

'Yes. France and Britain will become at the throats of each other. Each will blame the other for the catastrophe.'

I remembered what Hedge had said on our walk around Petersfield lake, the suggestion, more than a suggestion, I remembered, that the assassination was scheduled to take place on French soil, which had pleased Hedge immensely because then the British wouldn't be getting the opprobrium. That piece of information was nothing more than a red herring, as I had suspected it might be. I saw that now for sure. I saw something else as well: the terrible tragedy in the tunnel, the wrecking of the tunnel's credibility as a safe link between Britain and France was possibly of more importance basically then the deaths of the Foreign Ministers. The tunnel, that great symbol, that heroic status-enhancing endeavour, flagship as it were of the European dream, lying shattered, filled with bodies to help crack the myth of unity . . .

'And into the gap,' I said, following out my thoughts aloud now, 'steps the new Germany. The new Nazi Germany. Adolf Hitler reincarnated. Is that it?'

'Yes, that is it.' Heinrich got to his feet, knocking

over his hard, upright chair behind him as he did so. His
heels came together in a click. His right arm shot out at
an angle to his body. I saw his eyes alight with fervour,
with a kind of terrible, single-minded madness. He
shouted, '*Heil, Hitler!*'

I found it embarrassing. Ogmanfiller got to her feet
like Uncle Heinrich and also heiled Hitler. Not so
Polecat Brennan. He remained seated, smiling
sardonically. There were no particular politics about
Brennan. All that mattered to him was himself and the
acquisition of money and, overridingly, power. Power
to kill. He was that sort of man.

No more detail was gone into, either to do with the
tunnel or with the rise of Nazism from the ashes of
history. Brennan looked at his watch and said
something to Ogmanfiller about preparing to move out.
No mention was made of where to. Ogmanfiller left the
room; Brennan and Heinrich remained on guard. I was
wondering what part I was expected to play: there had
to be a reason why Brennan had at the last moment
extracted me from that well. There was a use for me
somewhere along the line; I wondered if there was any
connection there with Felicity.

The preparations for moving out didn't take very
long but I had time to think about Schmidt and his mad
idea of a return to Nazism. I heard those wildly cheering
mobs of prewar days, the heady excitement as the
Führer drove in style along the Unter den Linden,
beneath the Brandenburg Gate, acknowledging the

adulation, I heard him speak at the great rallies, heard the *Heils*, the singing of *Deutchland über Alles*, the screaming voice of Adolf Hitler as he approached the climax of his rant and, according to history, orgasmed in the same moment. I saw the club-footed Goebbels, the slimy von Ribbentrop, ex-wine salesman, Ambassador to the Court of St James, the fat Reichsmarschal Göring, gross and grotesque in his sky-blue uniform as Chief of the *Luftwaffe*, boasting with his Führer that not one bomb would fall on the Fatherland while Britain was obliterated by his bomber crews. I saw the other things: the pogroms, the concentration camps, the torture tactics of the Gestapo and the SS. And I saw the aftermath, when Adolf Hitler had died in his Berlin bunker – Dachau, Belsen, the heaps of bone-thin bodies, the living who were only just alive. I smelled the awful stench that had hung like a miasma. I saw the gas chambers where hundreds of thousands of innocents had died. It was all before my time, but from postwar accounts, newspapers, TV programmes, I could almost feel that it had been contemporaneous. Could it happen again? I believed it possible. The mass of the German people had not known those days, had not felt the evil for themselves. And there were very many men in present-day Germany who shared the views of Heinrich Schmidt, men who like him wanted nothing more than to see the Fatherland supreme again, marching to glory, and the only way they could see that happening was via a return to the dictatorship of Nazism.

My imaginings were interrupted by the return of

Ogmanfiller who, dressed now in a heavy, military-style greatcoat against the weather outside and lacking only the jackboots of the 1930s said that everything was ready.

Back through the warehouse, out into the snow. A different vehicle was waiting now: big car, a limousine, with a uniformed chauffeur and another man, another German by the look of him, by his side. The ropes had been removed from me before we went outside, but the guns were still very much with me though concealed in pockets. I was ordered into the back of the limousine to sit between Polecat Brennan and Schmidt. Ogmanfiller occupied a let-down seat.

Schmidt spoke into the intercom and the chauffeur started up. We rolled out of the yard; I noticed that there were still no overt signs of life. We went out the way I had come into Rinteln the day before, past the café, over the River Weser, past what had been the British military hospital, heading for Minden. Minden had ancient connections with British power. A battle had been fought here way back, against the Prussians, and it still figured in the regimental honours of the British Army, or what was left of it. Times had undergone drastic change. Unlike Heinrich Schmidt, there was nothing we could do about it.

In Minden the car pulled into the driveway of a biggish house. It stopped, and the man beside the chauffeur got out, went up a short flight of stone steps. As he reached a massive front door it opened and a man wearing a beret came out, lifted a hand towards Schmidt and came down to get into the car. He sat in another let-down seat alongside Ogmanfiller. After an initial greeting, uttered in French, he sat silent as the car got moving again.

French.

No names given, but I wondered if this was Louis X as referred to by Hedge on the Piccadilly Line. Louis X, representative of the hard Right of France.

Could be. It would fit.

From Minden, we seemed to be heading west, as I could see from the position of a weak sun that was struggling through thinning cloud cover as the snowfall ceased. West, for the coast maybe?

That could be an exit for Polecat Brennan. On the other hand, that was unlikely. Since the full impact of the EC had hit home, there was never trouble at the usual entry or exits – the land frontiers, the sea- and airports. Not exactly never. Not exactly in the case of Polecat Brennan, who was being watched for. And not in my case either, as Brennan's captive. Felicity or not, he wouldn't be relying on me not to snatch at freedom, and he certainly couldn't risk that now.

I was wrong. We drove through all that day, snacks provided by Ogmanfiller being consumed en route and shared with the two men in front. By dusk, which was early as the snow had cast its shadow again, we had entered a small town, Varel, which I knew was not far from Wilhelmshaven and the North Sea – or German Ocean as Schmidt would no doubt have had it.

Another yard, another warehouse.

We drove into the yard. Brennan said, 'This is where we stay till full dark.'

We left the limousine, which drove away as we went into the warehouse. I was tied again, tied to a chair and left with Ogmanfiller and her gun while Brennan, Schmidt, the supposed Louis X and the man who'd sat beside the chauffeur all went elsewhere. I looked at Ogmanfiller, at the dank hair, the thin, lanky body, the no-breasts. She was a real turn-off. So was Polecat Brennan. I wondered if they turned each other off or on. Did they sleep together, the awfulness of one acting to take away the horror of the other, the union of sex sublimating all aesthetic considerations? It would be a pretty gruesome sight. But there must be some reason why they stuck together and seemed amicable. Maybe it was just the money. And the power.

Time passed, quite a lot of time. Ogmanfiller had inexhaustible patience. She just sat there watching me closely, her automatic ever ready. She shifted about as though she wanted a pee after a while, but she didn't leave her post. When I said I wanted similar relief she said I would have to wait.

When it was full dark outside, Brennan and his thugs came back. Schmidt and the man from the front of the limousine were carrying something. It was a coffin. I was released from the chair. My wrists remained tied and a gag was placed over my mouth. I was lifted and put into the coffin and the lid was screwed down. I believe there was an air hole somewhere; I was able to

156

breathe as I was lifted and, apparently, carried outside. I was slid on runners into what was obviously a hearse, and since I was able to hear, dimly, a rattle of harness, a snort, and a hoof impatient on the yard stones, it had to be a horse-drawn one.

As soon as the coffin was positioned, we moved off.

I don't know how long or how far we travelled, but I did know later that it was to the coast, no doubt a lonely part of the coast, for when I was lifted again, and carried a little way, and once again set down, I could feel the coffin lifting and falling to the movement of a boat, a small one. Then the sound and beat of an engine, and more pronounced lifting and falling. I heard more sounds and realized, when electric light seeped into the coffin, that the screws were being released a little way to give me more air.

It was a long sea trip. A very long one. After a time I slept, still in the coffin. I don't know how many hours later, the coffin lid was removed altogether, the gag was also removed, and I was allowed to sit up. I was in what seemed to be a small cargo hold, currently empty of any legitimate cargo but containing what I had come to regard as the usual: Brennan, Ogmanfiller and the others, plus a tough-looking man in a blue seaman's jersey and a peaked, badgeless cap.

Brennan asked if I was all right.

'Just fine,' I said

'That's good. Sea's getting up.'

'I shan't be seasick,' I said.

'No. Of course. You were in the British Navy.' He gave me a funny sort of look, and caught the eye of the man in the seaman's jersey. I wondered if there was to be some connection, not yet revealed, between the rescue from the well and the fact that I'd served in the RN. But Brennan didn't elaborate and we all sat largely in silence, with me still sitting up in the coffin, feeling a prime example of a useless prat. In London, Max and probably Hedge would be doing their nuts, me not having contacted them for what would seem a long time, and was. I looked around. The man I believed to be Louis X was dark and lean and dangerous looking and was continually fondling a flick knife as though he couldn't wait to use it on someone; me, of course, if I should try anything on. He was fairly obviously French though apart from his initial greeting back in Minden I hadn't heard him utter. Obviously not the talkative kind of Frog. But French: the beret seemed to be a permanent fixture, he had a sort of Gallic shrug which he used a lot even though there was no verbal accompaniment and he had shifty eyes and chain-smoked Gauloises.

If he was indeed Louis X, then I fancied the whole principal cast was now assembled.

Except perhaps for one.

I decided to drop a pebble into the calm pool of silence. I asked, 'Where's Gerhardt von Defflinger-Zwickau?'

There was an immediate reaction: none of them liked that. Brennan, eyes like slits, said, 'What do you mean by that?'

158

I shrugged. 'What I said. Where is he?'

There was no direct answer. Brennan asked, 'What is known in London about — that name?'

I said I didn't know all that was known in London. I said once again that I'd been out of touch. Then I said, 'It's an obvious deduction, I'd have thought. The name over the factory. And the belle of the ball, right there in reception.'

'The belle of the ball?'

'Ogmanfiller,' I said.

Steenie Ogmanfiller came over and slapped my face hard. More blood from her rings. Louis X got up and joined her and extended the blade of his flick knife and laid the point against my throat. He spoke to Brennan, in very laboured English, speaking with an accent similar to the Franglais on *'Allo 'Allo*. He said, ''e ees bloakingg what 'e knows. You wish 'e speak?'

Brennan was about to answer, and I didn't know what his answer might have been, when there was a whistle from the deck and the man in the seaman's jersey left the hold and went up top. Brennan got to his feet and followed. A moment later he called down. The boat had made its landfall; and I was to be screwed down again.

No doubt more questions would be asked later. Now was obviously not the time.

I didn't know how long I'd been aboard that boat but although it felt as if it had plenty of power, it must have been in excess of twenty-four hours if, as I suspected, the destination was the south coast of England. Brennan would need to approach and land in darkness. To that end, if the snow from Germany had spread across the Channel, the weather would be much in his favour.

There was a rattle of deck gear as I was screwed back into the coffin, and I felt the easing of the engine. And just before the lid came down on me I picked up something familiar from my seafaring days: the sound signal from a lighthouse, the warning to shipping that a headland was not far off — the use of sound signals indicating that the visibility was right down low, just what Brennan wanted.

Not only that. I recognized the signal: the characteristic of the Dungeness light.

Dungeness: not so far from Folkestone. Not so far from the control system, the heart of Le Shuttle.

12

Journey's end. Also the beginning of the end for sundry persons: Pierre Monet and Humphrey Chatterton, or Brennan and his mob, one or the other. Or me. Or Felicity. Or both.

Of course, I didn't see our approach. But I was transferred from the German boat, in the coffin, to another boat, a boat under oars as I could tell from the creak of rowlocks and the grunt of the rowers, and the close sea sounds. Probably a fishing boat − and dead easy to land an illicit cargo on the total desolation that was Dungeness. The light was an unwatched one, automatic in its operation. And I was able to deduce from the odd remark, the odd loud curse, that the snow was falling thickly. Brennan had the luck with him, the devil's luck.

The boat touched on a shelving beach. I was lifted and carried. A vehicle was waiting. This vehicle drove off as soon as I had been embarked. It was all very smooth and efficient.

I was unpacked in what seemed to be a basement. No windows, and a stone-flagged floor, an old building. I assumed it would be Folkestone but I could have been wrong. (I wasn't, as it later transpired.)

Once again, they were all there. Still no Gerhardt von Defflinger-Zwickau, but probably as the big shot he was keeping in the background, all ready to emerge when the time was right for him, when the EC was in a turmoil and the private army of thugs (as I assumed the neo-Nazis would possess) were all set to come out as a mob to produce mayhem and thwart the forces of law and order. Or something like that. Widespread mobbery, organized mobbery with back-up and arms and the will to use them, is very hard to combat.

However, to my surprise, no questions. Nothing asked about why I had spoken of von Defflinger-Zwickau.

Why?

One clear answer: it was too late to bother. The time must be close now, the stage was set, and all they had to do was go for it.

With my assistance?

Yes.

Brennan, when I was again sitting up and listening, went into more details. As the two shuttles entered the tunnel, one from Calais with the French Foreign Minister aboard, the other from Folkestone carrying the British Foreign Secretary, Brennan's planted boyos, accredited and trusted staff in the control rooms at either end, would take over and operate the buttons to cause the ex-Folkestone shuttle to cross over into the path of the shuttle from Calais.

'And then bongk,' Louis X said, his cadaverous face coming alight for the first time. 'Such a big bongk.'

I said I had some questions.

'Go ahead,' Brennan said.

'Just two. First, how do your thugs take over without arms? There'll be electronic surveillance for one thing, and any metal object . . .'

'No guns,' Brennan said. 'Semtex.'

'A blow-up? What good would – '

'Not a blow-up, no. A threat.'

I laughed at that. 'One that wouldn't work – not unless your thugs are a suicide squad, Brennan.'

'How do you know they aren't?'

'Well – I don't. But human nature isn't like that. Not on behalf of some wet political ideal it isn't.'

Brennan smiled: he was so confident it wasn't true. He said, 'There is nothing to be gained by discussing the point. Now the second question you'd like to ask. Let me guess.' He appeared to ponder, quite a little act. Then he smiled and said, 'I've got it. You'd like to ask, what is your part in all this to be?'

'Yes,' I said.

'Your part will be quite important. Very important I should say. Now, I said, didn't I, that there would be no guns? That was not entirely accurate. There will be no guns *to start with* – when my operatives report for duty – and I should add that already I know the duty rosters, so there'll be no difficulty there. So, no guns at that stage. Not until you arrive. You'll have a quick-firing sub-machine-gun with you.' Brennan paused, smiling at me. 'You don't follow?'

I was looking and feeling blank. I said no, I didn't follow. Brennan explained. I was to demand entry through the security-guarded entry to the Folkestone control system, saying who I was and that I had to have entry to the control room as a matter of great urgency in order to safeguard the through passage of the Foreign Ministers. I would be assured of entry because before then I would have contacted Focal House by means of communication provided by guess who, Polecat Brennan himself. Naturally, I would be very circumspect in what I said, but I was to make it clear that I was on to something, unspecified, and it was essential that I should be admitted to the control room before the shuttles left from their respective ends of the tunnel. Focal House would ask, naturally, if the tunnel was after all concerned in the assassination threat. I would say yes, it was. But my entry to the control room would bowl the thing out, and those involved would be caught with their pants down. No, the visits and passages of the VIPs should not be negatived; that was important.

I would be given full details of my spiel later.

I asked, 'And then what?'

'Action, Commander Shaw. But first a warning: you will be covered by a long-range rifle with telescopic sights and you will be carrying with you a small transmitter – this transmitter will pick up anything you say to the security guards on the gate and transmit it back to the man with the rifle. One word out of place and you die. As does Miss Mandrake. Is this clear?'

'Clear enough,' I said. 'And when I get inside?'

'You cover everybody with your sub-machine-gun. You ensure that my operatives carry out their orders. The orders to operate the crossover.'

'Meaning you don't trust them after all?'

Brennan smiled. 'I never trust anybody,' he said. 'As for you . . . there is Miss Mandrake.' His eyes were cold steel, the steel of a killer.

Crazy; but capable of execution. Brennan's confidence was total. I took a deep breath. All the men were watching me. Ogmanfiller's eyes were what I would call joyful: the boyfriend had me in a real spot.

What I had to do was obvious enough: I had somehow to get in contact with Felicity. Then, somehow, I had to get away so as to alert Max. Max and the FO.

How − from a coffin?

I had no idea. I told myself there was always a way out waiting to be found. But that concept didn't really stand up to close inspection: what way out had there ever been from the condemned cell, other than via the hangman's noose?

There was no physical way out for me. Yet I had some bargaining power. It was clear enough that Brennan didn't wholly trust his agents in the control system. Maybe he hadn't quite the same hold over them as he had over me. Maybe they didn't have families, girlfriends, close ties. The men who'd worked for

Brennan over the years had certainly never been family men. Family life and Polecat Brennan didn't go together. I was obviously vital to the plan. I decided to use that bargaining power. It couldn't do any harm even if it didn't do any good.

So I said, 'You've forgotten something, Brennan.'

'What?'

'The possibility I might refuse.'

'In the circumstances, that's not really likely, is it?'

I said, 'On the contrary. I might find it a better prospect to die here and now, rather than let a hell of a lot of people down.'

'And Miss Mandrake?'

'She's been trained as an agent too,' I reminded him. 'She'll maybe see it the way I do − and take what comes.' I had in mind all the people who were going to die in the pile-up, in the shatter of carriages, in the fires that would inevitably follow the high-speed impact, in the stifling, fume-filled atmosphere right down beneath the layers of chalk and rock and marl below the Channel, among them winter-sport families soon setting out to board the shuttles. It didn't bear thinking about; but of course it meant nothing to Polecat Brennan. Just the same, I might be able to push him into a corner.

I said, 'If you want my co-operation, you're going to have to allow me something first.'

'What's that, then?'

'I want to see Miss Mandrake.'

'You'll see her afterwards.'

That was debatable. I didn't see either of us coming

out of this alive now. I knew Polecat Brennan rather too well. I said, 'I want to see her before. Not after.'

He sneered at that. I said I insisted. That was my condition. Otherwise, no dice.

Brennan, I believe, began to see that I meant it. And I was an essential part of his plan; the kidnap of Felicity had right from the start been a ploy to get hold of me. I saw that he was now in a quandary, and I bided my time.

The coffin had served its purpose: I could scarcely be delivered to the heavily guarded gates of the Folkestone control system by hearse and coffin. With wrists and arms tied and under many guns I was taken through a door and along a short passage to another part of the basement and shut into a small space with no window and, again, a stone slab floor.

No awareness of time; no means of knowing how far off zero hour was, but it couldn't be long now.

Brennan was, apparently, still making up his mind about my request to see Felicity.

What seemed an age later, the heavy door of the compartment was opened up. A light went on in the passage. Ogmanfiller stood there. Ogmanfiller, with inevitable gun.

'Out,' she said.

I moved out. 'Well?' I asked. 'Is the boyfriend going to play?'

'Just shut up,' she said. She prodded me with her automatic. I moved ahead of its snout, back along the passage. Back into the same room as before. Brennan was there; he was alone but for me and Steenie Ogmanfiller. He said, 'Request denied.'

'Right,' I said. 'In that case, it's not on. And that's final.' I really meant that, and was relieved that I'd made it plain. Felicity or no Felicity, I don't believe I could in any case have gone through with it. Far too many terrible deaths and injuries to have on my conscience for what would remain of my life. Also I still had that strong sense of duty, of loyalty to Max, which would be something Brennan wasn't capable of understanding. Duty, loyalty could never, with Brennan, count in the balance beside money and power.

But he did see that my mind was made up. And he did need me. Me — with the Felicity threat behind me keeping me to heel. He looked livid; but he conceded.

'All right,' he said, or rather snarled. He didn't like concessions. 'You'll have your meeting, but watch it. Watch it very, very carefully. Any funny business and you're both dead. You understand?'

'Understood,' I said. 'So how do we meet?'

'You don't meet yet. When you do, Miss Mandrake will be brought here.'

'When, Brennan?'

'When everything else is ready. Just before you make contact with Focal House.'

'And in the meantime?'

'In the meantime, you just wait.'

So I just waited, taken back by Ogmanfiller to that

small, dark, cell-like place. Once again, time passed. It couldn't be long now.

Once again the door was unlocked; once again by Ogmanfiller. Once again she said, 'Out,' and held her automatic steady. Once again, back to the room where I'd first been brought.

Brennan was still there, still alone. He looked ruffled. I was pleased to see that. I wondered what was up, but I didn't ask. I wouldn't have been told anyway.

Ogmanfiller said, 'Bring her in, do I?'

Brennan nodded. 'And the others.'

I felt a surge of emotion: I guessed that the 'her' was Felicity. In fact not so many days had passed since that night she'd been hooked away from the flat, but it seemed an age to me. I felt a shake in my hands, a tremble right throughout my body as Ogmanfiller left the room.

She was back inside a minute. Felicity, her hands and arms tied like mine, was with her. With her also were Louis X and Heinrich Schmidt. Felicity was pale and shaky but not, so far as I could see, harmed physically.

She was holding back tears. I could see that with half an eye. Unsteadily I uttered banalities. I said, 'Bear up, old darling. It hasn't happened yet.'

She nodded without speaking: she couldn't trust herself to speak, not yet. But she had plenty of guts and she'd had that rigorous training as an agent, a first-class agent of 6D2. She wouldn't break; I knew that.

I turned to Brennan. 'You've met your side of the

bargain,' I said. 'But there's something else. I want Miss
Mandrake to stay with me from now on out. Right?'

'For now, yes. Not all the way.'

I had to be content with that. Brennan said, 'Next the
contact. Focal House, by radio.'

The guns were still out. Louis X had his knife in his
hand and he was standing close to Felicity. I saw the
look in his eyes. He was fond of that knife, desperate
still for the chance to use it. Brennan was about to speak
again when there was a distant knocking, a peremptory
knocking on what was probably the front door of the
house.

There was an immediate reaction in the basement
room, a stiffening. Something was happening out of
schedule and none of them liked it. I saw that Brennan
was making up his mind: did he answer that knocking,
that very insistent knocking, or did he not? He couldn't
be sure it wasn't the cops. I felt a surge of excitement,
though truthfully I didn't believe it could be the police. I
could find no reason why they should pinpoint this
house. Bur whoever it was, the news might well at this
late stage be unwelcome to Polecat Brennan. There
might be a spanner in the works. I recalled that ruffled
look on Brennan's face when I'd been brought in just a
short while ago.

Brennan decided to answer: the knocking was going
on. He spoke to Ogmanfiller.

'Get it,' he said.

Ogmanfiller left the room, and we all waited.
Brennan was very tense.

The knocking stopped. Ogmanfiller had reached the door. Louis X was fingering his knife. The guns had moved closer to me. And to Felicity. I noticed Schmidt licking at his lips, very nervous now.

Footsteps came down a flight of stairs. Two lots. Ogmanfiller came back into the room. She was followed by a very tall man, an arrogant-looking man with a hard, square face and a stiff manner, very formal. German: there was no doubt about that. He could almost have been in the old uniform of the SS, Adolf Hitler's élite storm troopers.

This man stopped in the doorway, clicked his heels, and lifted his right arm in the Nazi salute.

'*Heil, Hitler!*' he said.

Schmidt seemed almost to genuflect as he, too, heiled Hitler. I'd been right about the newcomer's nationality; and now I was dead certain this was Gerhardt von Defflinger-Zwickau himself, probably, in his mind at any rate, potentially the new Führer of another German Reich, here in person to be around when the catalysing act, the assassination, took place.

But I couldn't for the life of me see why. I'd have thought he'd have waited on the other side of the Channel. England didn't seem to be likely to be a safe place after the balloon had gone up.

And I could see that Polecat Brennan was thinking along similar lines.

13

I revised my opinion of von Defflinger-Zwickau: I'd thought of the SS as being the old German élite; they were not. They only believed themselves to be so. Hitler's élite they certainly had been, but to the old German Army they had smelled pretty bad, almost as bad as the Gestapo. Gerhardt von Defflinger-Zwickau was of a different and genuine élite – the old German officer corps, probably a Prussian. Filled to the brim with old-fashioned German patriotism even though he was not of that generation: he looked to me no more than thirty-five or so. However, never mind the officer corps aspect, I didn't see much chivalry in that stony face. If there had been, he'd not have been a neo-Nazi.

His presence, his personality, filled the room.

Brennan, however, was no respecter of anybody at all; and he came out with his thoughts straightaway.

He said, 'I didn't expect you here and I don't like it. It's bloody dangerous. What's the big idea?'

Von Defflinger-Zwickau didn't like that. In good but accented English he said stiffly, 'I do not have to explain myself to you, Herr Brennan.'

Brennan smiled nastily. 'You do if you want this

thing to come off. You can't operate without me and you bloody know it, right?'

The German held onto his temper. I could see the effort, the cold anger in his eyes. He wouldn't like being beholden to a rat like Brennan; but of course he knew Brennan was right. He looked across at me and spoke to Brennan.

'This is the man Shaw?'

Brennan nodded. 'The one who's going to help us, yes.'

Von Defflinger-Zwickau stared me in the face. 'Swine,' he said. 'Swine, to betray your own country.' He had the Prussian ideas, all right. He turned back to Brennan: Brennan was an Irishman, so he wasn't betraying anything, except a few hundred innocents who would be aboard Le Shuttle. He asked, 'And the woman?'

He didn't mean Ogmanfiller. Brennan said briefly, 'The hostage.'

'Do they know our plans?'

'Partly,' Brennan said. 'Don't worry – they won't be passing anything on, that's for sure.'

'Very well.' Von Defflinger-Zwickau paused for a moment. 'I shall now tell you why I have come. It was necessary for me to come in person. I would not trust the radio contact. Not as things have turned out.' He paused again.

Brennan said, 'Well, go on.'

'Yes, I will go on, Herr Brennan. The G7 meeting – the venue has been changed, a last-minute decision

174

apparently. It is to take place in London. Do you realize the significance of this?'

Brennan obviously didn't; and neither did I. The G7 meeting, the confab between the various governments of the big boys of the world, had become an annual event. It had been scheduled to take place this year in Brussels. I didn't see what difference London made. But von Defflinger-Zwickau had more to say. Not only the venue but the timing also had been altered.

'To coincide with the exchange visit of the Foreign Ministers,' von Defflinger-Zwickau said.

'So?'

'Our Chancellor will be attending,' the German said.

Brennan grinned. 'Unlucky for some,' he said, 'and lucky for others. Case of two birds with one stone, right? Or three birds to be exact.'

'Not so. With the various missions will be large staffs of junior ministers, officials, secretaries. The German mission will rendezvous in Paris with the French mission, and all will travel that day with the Foreign Minister of France through the tunnel from Calais to Folkestone. Do you see?'

'No,' Brennan said flatly. 'If you want – '

'I do not kill Germans, Herr Brennan.'

Brennan was furiously angry. He stormed about the room: the German was adamant. Brennan said he was nothing but a bloody hypocrite; he couldn't ever gain what he wanted, which was ultimately power for his neo-Nazis in a riven Europe – he couldn't achieve that without killing plenty along the way. Von Defflinger-Zwickau made what I considered was the perfectly valid point that among the German delegation to the G7 meeting were a number of high-ranking persons who were in sympathy with his ideas and would be essential to the eventual consolidation of his schemes. He said they were vital.

He would not kill them, period.

Brennan seethed. 'So what do you suggest?'

'Some other way must be found.'

'Not at this stage, boyo! Not at this stage. Look, the whole thing's set up to go and there's not long now. There's just no goddamn time to muck around now.' Brennan was seeing his rewards vanishing into thin air and he was beside himself with frustration. 'It's no good, it can't be done and that's flat!'

'I will not kill those Germans,' von Defflinger-Zwickau said, his voice a whiplash. He smacked a hand against his thigh, just as though the hand had held a German officer's cane. 'An alternative must be found.'

'Okay,' Brennan spat out. 'Then you're the one that's going to have to dream it up. I've done my part, right?' His chest heaved with anger. 'Go on, suggest something, why don't you?'

It was Ogmanfiller who stepped in where no one else seemed inclined to stick their necks out. She said, 'This G7. The French and German bunch. Do they go in the same shuttle as the Frog, the French Foreign Minister I mean?'

Von Defflinger-Zwickau said no, they didn't. That

cross-visit was still on as a separate journey. The symbolism of the tunnel was still there, was still considered important, especially to the French who loved their nationalism and believed in their hearts that the tunnel concept was all their own, Britain only a minor participant. The combined delegations would go through the tunnel after the exchange shuttle.

Brennan pumped out a long breath of relief. 'Well, then,' he said, 'that makes it okay, doesn't it? The shuttle with the Foreign Ministers goes up, the next one is held back, right?'

'Not necessarily so,' von Defflinger-Zwickau said. 'I do not know precisely *which* shuttle will be used. If it follows close behind, then it will be involved in the smash – '

There's a safety factor,' Brennan interrupted. 'An interval between the shuttles – '

'How long, the intervals?'

Brennan shrugged. 'Fifteen minutes. Plenty of time to bring the next shuttle to a stop.'

Von Defflinger-Zwickau was still not keen, but in the end Brennan talked him round and got his agreement to let the plans go ahead – subject to one proviso. Brennan would remain in the Folkestone hideout. With von Defflinger-Zwickau, who would be armed. Brennan would not be armed. If anything went wrong in the tunnel, if disaster should come to the Germans in the following shuttle, Brennan would die.

Brennan raised strenuous objections. There was, he

said, no possibility of anything going wrong. He had his planted stooges in the control system. All would be well.

'Then you will have no reason to worry, Herr Brennan.'

'But I – '

'There will be no argument,' von Defflinger-Zwickau said. 'I have stated what I wish and there is no more to be said.'

Brennan had to accept that. With a bad grace, he caved in. He spoke to me. 'It's going to be up to you,' he said.

I took his point. He would be expecting me, armed as I would be, to take full charge in the control room and ensure that the following shuttle was stopped in time. I doubted if he was at all happy to have his life to some extent in my hands. But, of course, there was always Felicity.

Brennan said, 'The contact goes ahead. You'll still speak to your HQ.'

Then followed a briefing as to what I was to say. And, of course, what I was not to say. Felicity would be present throughout that radio contact. And I knew what that meant.

Brennan's setup was no doubt on the phone; but phones were too risky. And likewise the radio contact: it would not be made from the house. There was the car that had brought us from Dungeness, and it would be used for the contact.

So we went out to the car. It was night once again, no snow here but rain, buckets of it. The streets ran with it and there was no one walking and very little traffic. The house was a big one, as I saw as I emerged from the basement area with Heinrich Schmidt's gun against my spine. We came out onto the Leas, a broad clifftop walk above the English Channel. In the distance to the southwest I picked out the light signal from the Dungeness lighthouse. The visibility in the rain was not brilliant but it was good enough now for the sound signals not to be needed by the ships at sea.

We drove out of the town, heading west. Along the way, somewhere short of Hythe, I believe, we stopped. Brennan was driving; von Defflinger-Zwickau hadn't interfered, hadn't made him stay behind. It wasn't likely Brennan would dirty his own doorstep now by trying to get out from under the German's grip.

'Right,' Brennan said. I was in the back with Schmidt and Louis X. Schmidt had his silenced gun; the Frenchman had that knife. Felicity was in the front passenger seat and the knife was now laid against the back of her neck. I saw her flinch instinctively as the point pricked her skin. Brennan was getting his radio equipment set up and when it was ready he passed a microphone to me. The contraption worked like a radio telephone. Brennan didn't ask me for the Focal House coded number. He knew it already. Trust him.

He keyed in the number. I'd been told already as part of the briefing that I was not to ask for Max himself. I was to speak to the duty officer, using my personal identification so that the authenticity of my call would not be doubted. I was to be brief, was not to answer

179

questions. I was in a desperate hurry; I was to cut short any back-talk.

I took a deep, deep breath. Waiting for Focal House to answer, I knew that I could stop the whole thing dead by uttering just one word: abort. When that reached Max, he would immediately take the point. The FO would be contacted and the wires would become red-hot between London and Paris and the exchange visit would be called off. I could by that one small word save a hell of a lot of lives. But Felicity would die before my eyes. There still had to be another way.

Focal House answered.

I gave my identification code. 'Listen good,' I said. 'I've not much time − I'm in a spot.' That part was very true. 'I'm on to something.' The duty officer would know the score, know what my assignment was: every watch officer was always provided with the details of a field man's assignment. 'I need entry to the Folkestone control at 0600 Thursday − see to that. The result'll be a total roundup of the villains. Meantime, no info to be passed on beyond Focal House. That's vital. So is this: the exchange visit is not repeat not to be negatived. I want a clean sweep. Understood?'

'Understood. Why − '

'Out,' I said, and Brennan switched the set off. I was bathed in sweat. My hands were shaking. I'd done it now, and no doubt von Defflinger-Zwickau had been right: swine was a fitting word. But Felicity was still alive.

Louis X withdrew his knife. Brennan turned the car

and we drove back into Folkestone.

I was put back in the cell-like place I'd been in earlier.
Felicity was with me. Our wrists and arms were still tied.
We spoke in whispers, and not about any plans I might
or might not have − I hadn't in fact. The cell was most
probably bugged and I wasn't going to take chances of
inadvertently aiding Brennan by any talk about the job
in hand, or about Max or Focal House. All I did was to
ask Felicity how she'd been treated, where she'd been
held, that sort of thing.

She didn't know where she'd been held. It had been
the black bag treatment, like me. But she spoke of the
use of the whip, just the once in fact, largely just for my
benefit she believed. Food and drink at intervals, acute
discomfort, bare floors, no bedding. Polecat Brennan
hadn't been there all the way though, as of course I
knew. When he had been there, things had been a lot
worse. There had been questioning and threats and
pain. Cigarette burns on her body, where they didn't
show normally. Polecat Brennan had seen to her in
person and had enjoyed it. At one stage she'd been
stripped and tied down to a sort of rack, and her body
had been stretched. I hoped I would find a way of
killing Polecat Brennan. Legally.

The night passed. We'd both slept in the end, fitfully.
Breakfast was brought − cornflakes with cold milk,
toast, stewed tea. This was brought by Ogmanfiller, who
fed us with a spoon and tilted the teacup against our lips.
'Have a good night, did you?' She smirked. 'Not

much chance with your hands tied, I guess.'

We didn't respond, didn't rise to her. What would have been the point? When she'd finished feeding us, she took her disgusting acne away and left us in peace. We stayed in the cell all day, in the pitch darkness. We heard things going on around us and overhead and were left to wonder what it all meant. I found myself thinking, not of Pierre Monet or Humphrey Chatterton or the EC, but of the ordinary people who would at this very moment be making ready to drive down to Folkestone early next morning to embark aboard the doomed shuttle; or taking the train from Waterloo right through to Paris. I hadn't established whether or not the Paris-bound shuttle would be a train shuttle or a drive-on. I did know the two were never mixed, it was one or the other. Whichever it was, there would be those happy innocents, packing up, looking forward perhaps to a ski-ing holiday, none of them having the remotest idea of what lay ahead. Happy and carefree, or travelling on business, anticipating deals with fellow Europeans, not knowing just how the cards had already been dealt.

A long, long day. We had no idea of the time. Not until the door was opened up and a light came on in the passage and there was Brennan with Heinrich Schmidt and Ogmanfiller. Brennan said it was midnight and I was to be equipped with the miniature transmitter that would relay back to a gunman, waiting with his telescopic-sighted, long-range rifle, anything I might say out of turn when I approached the gates of the Folkestone control.

I'd been wondering about that. Why didn't I just chuck it away? But that of itself would probably cause the thing to give the warning.

Anyway, I soon found out that I wouldn't be able to chuck it away.

Brennan produced a small capsule. It was like a cod-liver-oil capsule, only a shade larger.

He told me to open my mouth. Schmidt urged obedience with his gun. So I obeyed. Brennan shoved the capsule into my mouth and then immediately seized my jaws and held them clamped together, hard. The capsule went down quite easily by involuntary movements of my throat.

That was that; they withdrew, but not before Ogmanfiller had had her say.

'You won't get rid of it,' she said. 'That's to say, you won't like *pass* it. Why? Because when the outer casing melts, which it does fairly fast, then small sort of wings come out. Metal projections, like scales, I guess. Know what? It'd be like trying to pull a herring the wrong way.'

She left, laughing. She had enjoyed her little simile. Brennan, just before he too left us, said I would be required at 0600. 'Have a good sleep meantime,' he said, and banged the door shut and locked it.

Just six hours left.

They came back just before 0600, and found me awake. I hadn't slept; my mind had been, still was, too active. I had to think of a way — not only for Felicity and the shuttle passengers and, I suppose, the EC, but also to redeem myself. I had no wish to go down in history as a swine.

There was a change in the plans: because von Defflinger-Zwickau was adamant that Brennan was to remain in the house with him, someone else had to stand by outside the control complex with the long-range telescopic-sighted rifle. The someone else was to be Heinrich Schmidt. Felicity remained behind. I couldn't shake Brennan on that. Louis X with knife went with me and Schmidt. The driver was a man I'd not seen before.

We went out westwards, past the tunnel's exhibition centre and the ramps where the cars were loaded aboard the shuttles, past the main railway tracks running to and from the yawning entries to the tunnels. In front, Schmidt switched on the radio and we listened to the early news broadcasts. It was to be full fig in London for the state arrival of the French Foreign Minister and now, of course, for the previously unexpected arrival of the heads of state attending the G7 summit. It must have been quite a headache, taking into account the advanced date which wouldn't have been made known until almost the last minute. A royal personage would meet the trains at the London terminus, there would be immense preparations in hand at Chelsea Barracks where the guardsmen would be polishing boots and buttons, in Knightsbridge Barracks where the household cavalry's horses would be similarly buffed up for the great occasion. Once again I thought of the ordinary British travelling public, soon to get up for what would for many of them be their last day on earth.

Max would almost certainly have been at Focal House right through the night. Wondering about me. Furious that I'd not spoken to him personally when I'd called the duty officer. He would know that the whole thing was now in my hands. The next few hours could bring disaster. Max would have been in a real tizzy when he got the news about the summit coming to London, this day of all days. I guessed he would have argued against it in high places. Likewise, no doubt, Hedge. But it seemed neither of them had pulled it off.

But whatever might be the Foreign Office view that nothing would happen in the tunnel, someone must surely have ticked over that it would be a sensible precaution to put further checks on the staff manning the control system. I put this point out to Heinrich Schmidt.

He said, 'Yes.'

'So?'

'We have no worries. Our men were well selected long ago; they have unimpeachable backgrounds.'

'On the surface.'

'On the surface, yes. Also underneath. And they have passed all the securities.'

No doubt they had. It wouldn't have been all that difficult. Security sounds fine, but it's never watertight. If it had been, we wouldn't have had all the spies that had acted against our interests over so many years since the end of the last war. Nor on a lesser scale would there have been, and still be, so many moles in Whitehall, or in commercial companies, stealing secrets and passing them on to interested parties. Security was largely a sick joke. People can always be fooled and probes blunted. And, as I'd reflected so often before, Polecat Brennan was no fool. Neither, from what I'd seen of him, was Gerhardt von Defflinger-Zwickau. No fool at all, and clearly dedicated. A single-minded man. Like Adolf Hitler himself: today Germany, tomorrow the world.

We drove on, north of the town now, to what seemed like a kind of Armageddon. Currently, I couldn't find any way to make Brennan's plans come unstuck.

Schmidt imparted some information. We had stopped now, in a lay-by out of sight from the control complex, and Schmidt turned in his seat to speak to me.

He said, 'The French Foreign Minister boards the train in Paris at 10 a.m. British time. At 11.35 he will enter the tunnel at Calais. Ten minutes after this, the British Foreign Secretary will enter the tunnel from Folkestone. The trains will be crossed for impact at the crossover point nearest Britain. The impact will come at approximately 11.50 hours. I tell you this so that you will know what action to expect from the control operators.'

'*Your* operators.'

'Yes.'

I looked at the clock in the car's console. The time was just after 7 a.m. It seemed a longish interval. I asked why this was. Schmidt shrugged and said, 'A precaution only.'

'Against what?'

'Against leakages. If there is suspicion about the house, then it is better that you are not in it. It is better that you are in the car.'

It sounded a little screwy to me. I asked, 'But what about Brennan and von — '

'They are able to look after themselves. But if you had been contained in the house — '

'Right,' I said. 'I get it.'

I worried myself sick about Felicity. It was unlikely, I thought, that anyone would have ticked over about the Folkestone house. But if they had, and if Felicity was caught as it were in the crossfire . . . . no good thinking along those lines. But by now I was convinced I would never see Felicity again.

There were things that would be taking place which I wasn't currently in a position to know about but which I could assess easily enough. There would be massive security in London, much more so now that the G7 was about to take place. Those responsible would have been caught on the hop over that and they'd be working overtime on it. Police everywhere, marksmen on the roofs around the rail terminal, marksmen all along the ceremonial route, all the way to Whitehall or maybe Buckingham Palace — I didn't know which would be the first port of call for the VIPs. Parking restrictions, bomb searches, drains examined and the covers sealed,

waste bins turned inside out, stray packages given a
going over by the bomb squads, Scotland Yard and MI5
leaving no stone unturned, all that sort of thing.
Stringent security also along the route to be taken to the
terminus by the welcoming royal.

And all concerned knowing very well that all the hoo-
ha could be overturned in seconds by one man in a
window with a long-range rifle. Which, I guessed, was
the way the authorities would still be assessing the
threatened assassination and never mind my enforced
message to 6D2. The conventional way. That, or an
undiscovered bomb somewhere close to the route.

Not the tunnel, oh no.

London would be all ready. Pierre Monet would be
well guarded, his entourage stiff with plain-clothes men,
all marksmen. In London.

And only I knew that it wasn't going to happen in
London.

Time passed. I was clock-watching now as the
seconds and the minutes ran down to disaster. At a little
after 8.30 Schmidt got out of the car, went round to the
boot and brought out a basket. Coffee and ham rolls
and fish-paste sandwiches. Probably prepared by
Ogmanfiller.

Like any family party, we picnicked.

At 9 a.m. Schmidt put the basket back in the boot and
came back inside with his long-range rifle, stripped
down and cased. He began to assemble it, and the driver
started up and we moved out of the lay-by.

14

Schmidt had in fact brought two cases from the boot. The second one, I assumed, contained the quick-firing sub-machine-gun that I was to take with me into the control complex. I was right. When he had assembled his own rifle. Schmidt assembled mine. Then he explained what was to happen. The car would be driven past the gateway with its security guard and would stop, out of sight of the gate, beyond a concealing bend in the road. I would disembark and run back for the gate. With my arrival already announced by Focal House, I would have no need to go into any explanations as to, for instance, why I'd turned up on foot. If necessary I could speak of an emergency and no time to be lost. I would ask for a guide to the control room, the centre of operations.

That would be all. In the meantime, Schmidt and Louis X would have driven to a vantage point overlooking the complex and there they would wait with Schmidt's telescopic sights trained on me as I made my entry. I saw a little hope in that I might be able to speak out of turn if I was able to put a part of the buildings between myself and Schmidt's rifle, but, of course, that was not to be, as Schmidt, almost as though he had read my mind, remarked.

He said, 'All has been very thoroughly reconnoitred, of course. You will be in sight all the way from the gate to the control bunker.' And he added remindingly, 'If the little bug in your inside registers anything I do not like, then you die immediately.'

So, of course, did Felicity. But I spotted a last-minute dichotomy. If I died before I got to the control room, what happened to my part in the proceedings? Who, in my absence, would ensure that the trains crossed, that the planted operators didn't get cold feet, or — more likely — that the genuine personnel got wise just in time and took over the control? Brennan's people, and this had been made quite clear to me, had no weapons. Only the Semtex; and the function of the Semtex, if it had to be used, had not been explained.

I put the question to Schmidt.

He said, 'That is taken care of.'

I didn't doubt it. But I asked, 'How?'

'If you have to die,' Schmidt said, 'the news will quickly reach the control room, will it not?' It would; any shooting, any death inside the complex, would be very big news indeed. Schmidt went on to explain. He said the last-resort method would be put into operation. And the last resort was the Semtex.

I said I didn't get it. Schmidt said, with a laugh, that I didn't need to. Obviously, I was to be kept in the dark in regard to some matters. Schmidt wouldn't say any more. But I believe he saw no reason to expect to have to use the last resort. I wasn't going to say anything out of turn, he believed. And he was dead right. I wasn't. I had to live to get inside the control room. And Felicity was still in that anonymous house in the town.

I was still hamstrung.

In another lay-by, the car stopped again. Schmidt was keeping a close eye on the clock. The time was now 9.34 and we had moved away from the railway tracks, a little north.

From where we parked I had a view of the tunnel entry and loading bays for the cars, coaches and lorries. The area was busy with numbers of cars being guided into the car shuttle. The lorry park was equally busy. Cars and lorries went through in separate shuttles, the train passengers from the London terminus went separately again, sitting tight in the carriages for the tunnel passage. It was all very efficient and it was obviously a gigantic load of work and responsibility for the controllers. Split-second timing in drawing up the schedules, a rigid adherence to timing thereafter, one slip and there could be chaos.

There was going to be chaos.

I couldn't calculate how many trains would run into each other once those particular shuttles from London and Paris had been put onto their collision course. The control room, in the hands of Brennan's mob, wouldn't be stopping to sort it out. And the loyal men, the genuine staff, would need to react very fast indeed. If they were allowed to. And the Brennan mob? Schmidt, or had it been von Defflinger-Zwickau — or Brennan himself — had said the plants were dedicated men prepared for death, a suicide squad, real *kamikaze* stuff. That might be so. For my money, however, they would try to fight their way out. And that might be the way the Semtex came in. Or one of the ways.

And me, when the thing was done? I would have that sub-machine-gun and I would use it.

Like Schmidt, I watched the clock: 9.48, and the little green numbers clicking over inexorably.

Ten a.m. 10.01 . . . At 11.50 the trains would meet. Less than two hours to go. The day was cold, cold rain was lashing down, but I had begun to sweat. There was a fug in the car, not helped by Louis X's Gauloises. No one was speaking now; there was enormous tension in the car. Schmidt's hands trembled slightly as he reached out to wipe the windscreen clear of the mist-up, using a yellow duster. Every now and again the driver switched the engine on and used the wipers, back and front, to clear the rain.

Ten twenty-five and we waited still.

At 11.10 Schmidt spoke to the driver, and the car pulled away, turned, headed back towards the town and the tracks.

At 11.28 precisely we went past the complex entry and moved on around the bend which Schmidt had spoken of earlier. We stopped. We were something like three hundred metres from the gate. I was told to get out. The sub-machine-gun was put into my hands. I resisted the urge to spray the car with lead: that would achieve nothing beyond three deaths, it wouldn't stop what was going to happen and it was Polecat Brennan I wanted in my gun-sight.

'Remember all you've been told.' Schmidt said. Then the door was slammed and the car went off, moving very fast and accelerating. It vanished at a roundabout. I carried out my orders. I made back for the gate at a run.

There was no trouble at the gate. Focal House had done its stuff. I just said who I was and that was it. The picket gate beside the road barrier was opened and in I went. I asked, as ordered, for a guide to the control room. This was accorded me. I followed the guide, aware of the distant, concealed rifle with its sights on my back. We entered a building and I was safe from Schmidt. But Felicity wasn't safe from Brennan.

I entered the control room. It was dark, with green lights winking, as it seemed, all over. Ahead of me were television screens covering the tracks from both directions. Below the screens were banks of dials and buttons with men sitting motionless and intent at the consoles.

Someone approached me. The time, as I saw from a big digital clock, was 11.35. Pierre Monet would be entering the tunnel from the Calais end. In ten minutes' time the British Foreign Secretary would enter the Folkestone tunnel. In fifteen minutes the two trains would meet as the crossover was ordered from the men at the consoles.

And I was there to see that that was what happened. Me — the only one who could in fact prevent it happening now. I could do it so easily, no trouble at all. I had the gun; no one else had. But if I did it, I signed Felicity's death warrant.

It was as all this was running through my head that I realized who the man was who had approached me. It was dark except for those flickering green lights, and my eyes hadn't immediately adjusted.

The man was Max.

To say I was shocked would be to understate it. But perhaps I shouldn't have been. Max could easily enough have put two and two together after my message had reached him and here he was. Maybe he'd had a battle with Hedge and the rest of the Establishment, hadn't won out and had decided to act in person and unofficially.

There was no time to go into the whys and wherefores now.

Max came up close. I sensed his unspoken query: something had gone wrong in the atmosphere.

At this stage I had to risk the bug. I whispered in his ear, 'I don't know who's which.' I told him what my orders were, my orders from Brennan and Schmidt.

Max took it all in, fast. He said, 'Better carry out the orders for now. As to who's genuine and who isn't — we'll just have to watch carefully — all we can do. Situation's too knife-edge, too damn delicate to interfere and maybe cause a worse cockup.'

I nodded. Another man was coming towards us, arms akimbo. In the many green glows I caught a glimpse of the expression on his face, puzzled, wary.

Following Max's advice, I went into my act.

I held them all covered – everybody, the whole control setup. I warned them not to move, not to interfere with each other, just to do what they'd been told.

No one moved. Max remained by my side. We watched the figures moving, second by second, on that digital clock. We watched the television screens, watched the progress of the shuttle carrying the British Foreign Secretary. The train bringing Pierre Monet and his staff from Calais was not yet on the other screen.

I wondered how far behind Pierre Monet the G7 lot would be. The German Chancellor, the various presidents with their inflated staff backup. There would be hundreds of secretaries, minions of all sorts speeding with the big boys into the tunnel at some point in time. I thought of Polecat Brennan, sweating it out in company with Gerhardt von Defflinger-Zwickau, who could be relied upon to deal with Brennan if his friends in the German entourage were killed. Polecat Brennan was getting some of his own medicine now.

The seconds ticked away.

By the digital clock, 11.47 and three minutes to go.

Just three minutes. With Max, I watched closely to try to find some sort of reaction from the operators at the consoles, some sign of nerves or tension. I moved in closer behind them. I could detect nothing. The scene was calm, unhurried. On the television screen, the Foreign Secretary's shuttle rushed on, not yet, so far as I could tell, diverted into the crossover tunnel.

11.48.

Two minutes. Sweat was pouring down my face.

At 11.49 I saw one of the operators half turn in his seat and reach towards a button set some twelve inches to his right. I felt the pressure of Max's hand on my shoulder. He spoke in a whisper. 'Get him,' he said, and he added, 'I'm bloody sorry,' and I knew he meant Felicity.

I squeezed the trigger of the sub-machine-gun, just briefly. There was a yelp of pain, the hand moved away from the button. I think I saw the spurt of blood. Neither Max nor I could say for sure whether or not the man had reached for the crossover control. But the train on the television screen was moving on.

The air in the compartment was sharp, acrid with gunsmoke. No one had moved: the threat from my sub-machine-gun was now very plainly for real.

The next minute something happened on the television screen. The image of the shuttle vanished. In its place I saw a great upsurge, an outrush of smoke and flame and flying debris, some of it great chunks of concrete. Then the screen went blank. As it did so a telephone rang, a sound of extreme urgency in the circumstances, and a light glowed above the instrument.

Max called out, 'Leave it,' and moved across to answer it himself.

15

Max put down the telephone. 'Explosion in an access shaft,' he said briefly. 'At the bottom, near the track. There've been casualties.' Then he added, as though he'd been savouring the moment, 'The shuttle's all right.'

The Semtex? The last resort? If that was what it was, then it didn't seem to have worked.

But I'd had that thought a little prematurely. In almost the same instant as the thought came into my mind, one of the operators spoke. I hadn't seen him or anyone else move a hand or a muscle. Maybe I'd been less attentive than I should have been after Max had said the shuttle was safe. Whatever, the man who now spoke had done the trick. Calmly he said, 'The shuttle is now in the crossover tunnel.' And then he added, '*Heil, Hitler*!'

After that, the sorting of the sheep from the goats, all of them covered by my gun, was comparatively easy. Max sorted out the man in charge. Urgent telephone calls were made while the TV screen now showed the shuttle from Calais with the French Foreign Minister aboard

coming into the picture, hurtling on to impact with the
shuttle moving into the north running tunnel. I herded
the goat section into a corner while the sheep under the
senior duty controller stayed at their consoles and tried
to cope with approaching disaster. As a result of one of
the phone calls a squad of armed police with plain-
clothes men piled in through the door and took over the
villains. When they'd gone, apparently not in the least
worried but wearing smiles of self-congratulation, I had
words with Max.

'That,' I said, 'is my lot. I've made a cockup of it and
I'm sorry. I can't say more.'

'We'll sort out the blame later,' Max said. 'For now,
I'll just say you haven't made all that much of a cockup
and it may turn out all right. I gather they may be able
to stop the shuttle in time. It's on a knife-edge at the
moment. And I know what you want. So go and do it –
and the best of luck. I love that girl too, believe it or
not.'

Max looked almost tearful; or maybe it was just the
effect of the green light.

I had only a rough idea where Brennan's safe house
was; and Folkestone was a biggish area to cover.
Brennan might not be there anyway, most probably
wasn't, he'd have scarpered with von Defflinger-
Zwickau the moment he got the word that his boyos had
gone into apparently satisfactory action.

On the other hand, maybe he wouldn't know that yet.
Maybe he needed to wait for the news to break on the

radio. Until then, he might stay put, waiting. And by the same token, the chances were that Felicity would be safe for the time being. I prayed that might be so. And before I left the complex on a Brennan hunt I implored Max to hold the news just as long as humanly possible, whatever the ultimate reports from the track might be: disaster or boundless relief.

Another thing I arranged with Max, for what it might be worth, was a police cordon to be thrown around Folkestone. Of course, it could never be drawn really tight around such a large area, but at least roadblocks could be set up on all exits and the coast could be put under surveillance by police helicopters, backed up if necessary by the navy. It would at least put a few obstacles in Brennan's way, and in any case it was all that could be done.

That fixed, I was loaned a car by the Eurotunnel authorities and I drove fast into Folkestone. I was looking for somewhere not too far from the Leas, somewhere in the seaward fringe of the town. On that earlier drive out from Brennan's safe house I'd not picked up any road names and all I had to go on was the general look of the buildings. Mostly very big houses, four or five storeys plus basements, one looking much like another, and probably almost all of them now converted into hotels or flats.

I hadn't gone very far before I realized I had a tail, and the tail was the car carrying Schmidt and Louis X. Of course, they would have been watching out from their vantage point that covered the control area.

And I didn't like the implications: if they recognized me they would assume that something hadn't gone according to plan. Otherwise, why was I exiting? My orders from Brennan had been that once the trains had impacted and there was panic throughout the system, I was to stay put. From that point on, my future hadn't been gone into.

I thought fast.

With that tail, I wasn't going to be able to do any investigating around Folkestone. Not unless I could shake it and just then the prospects didn't look good. The tail was fast, had more power than my loaned car, and the driver was skilful.

However, for once luck was with me.

I was waved down by a police roadblock. The police had gone into action very fast. Two vehicles were drawn across the road, leaving only a small space between.

I braked, skidded to a halt. 'Commander Shaw,' I said, as an armed constable approached. '6D2'.

'From the — '

'I've just left the control complex,' I said. I was looking in my rear-view mirror. The tail had braked, turned and was going back the way it had come. I said, 'It's vital you get word through to have that car stopped. It contains two of the villains most concerned in this. And I'd like to be let through pronto.'

An inspector, also armed, had joined the constable. I repeated what I'd just said and asked, 'Is there any further news from control?' Never mind that I'd only just left: things could be happening very fast now.

'Nothing that I know of,' the inspector said.

I nodded. 'Will you let me through, please?' I asked.

He wanted identification. By this time I had none, and I said so. Other cars were now coming up behind, a queue was forming. The inspector was not a fast-thinking man. I was desperate to get on. While he was scratching his head and trying to think up his response, I suggested as patiently as possible that he might make radio telephone contact either with his HQ or, if possible, direct with the shuttle control where he would speak to Max. That seemed to ring a bell with him; he walked away to one of the police cars and when he came back he said it was all right for me to proceed. I think his decision was possibly hastened, if that is the word, by the increasing size of the queue, with the drivers in some cases tooting their horns. I reckoned the Prime Minister had produced a Charter to do with the police, and this was one of the times when it behove the police to observe it. Anyway, one of the blocking cars was shifted a little and I was waved through the gap.

Too much bloody time wasted, I thought savagely, but at least there was no more tail.

Any sort of a search through Folkestone was a dead duck, hopeless from the start. I began to think, as I sat in that loaned car on the Leas, looking to seaward where snow clouds were once again moving in, that the only way to play it was somehow or other to flush Brennan out into the open. How, was the problem. And when he was flushed? The police cordon might hold him but I hadn't much real hope that it would. Polecat Brennan would be too crafty for that and there were so many ways out. For a start, I thought, the sea would offer him the best prospect. Especially if, as seemed likely, the weather closed in again and a fresh snowfall grounded the helicopters. One passed overhead just at that moment and went slowly along the Leas. I could see the police personnel in the cabin, scanning the ground beneath.

I had the car radio switched on. I heard a news broadcast; there was nothing at all about the shuttle, no references whatever. Just a resumé of earlier bulletins, that the French Foreign Minister was due to arrive and would be met et cetera et cetera.

Would he arrive?

If he didn't arrive, what would the news broadcasters say?

That would be the moment when Brennan would get the word one way or another. That would be when his balloon went up. His and Felicity's —

My thoughts went back to the sea. Brennan, and probably even more so von Defflinger-Zwickau and Schmidt, would want out. Out, across the Channel — not perhaps to France, but to the safer shores of Germany. Certainly that was where von Defflinger-Zwickau and Heinrich Schmidt would want to be if the plan had worked out. And Ogmanfiller? She would go where Brennan went, presumably. Well — good luck to her: Brennan was going right for the high jump when I got hold of him.

Wishful thinking.

I hadn't got a scent of him.

I stayed where I was, in the car with the radio still switched on. And it was from that stationary position on the Leas that I had my second stroke of luck. Or I thought it was at the time. I saw the tail car, the one from earlier. Its occupants didn't see me; the car was passing along the seafront, turning left out of an approach road, and I was parked along the other way and more or less concealed by some bushes.

I started up and followed at a discreet distance. It was reasonably certain they meant to rendezvous with Brennan, if not drive straight for the safe house. Which wouldn't be safe any more if they did, though they might not know that.

The thrill of the chase came back to me once again. No more indecision.

As I moved off, I heard the next BBC news broadcast. There was a snatch of the *Marseillaise*, tinned, I think, from the studio. London was all gay abandon, the welcoming royal had been cheered along the route from Buckingham Palace, the Foreign Minister of France had set foot on the red carpet.

The shuttle had come through. I would get the whole story later from Max. But in the meantime, a vengeful Polecat Brennan and a furiously disappointed Gerhardt von Defflinger-Zwickau plus Heinrich Schmidt would be moving out.

But fast.

Thinking about fast, I put on more speed. I still had
that car in view and I just must not lose it. Easier said
than done as, with other cars now between us, it turned
left at the end of the Leas, heading it seemed for the
town centre. Then left again, and then a right-hand
turn.

I saw it stop. It pulled in behind another car, a big
Volvo estate. I stopped myself some distance behind.
We were in a big square with a central garden, winter-
bleak. Tall houses all around, all of them, as I'd
thought earlier, either hotels or flats. They'd once been
elegant, single-family houses, with wealthy owners or
tenants. They were still elegant but there was a
difference, the subtle difference that came with multiple
occupancy and the fact of a coach party disembarking
outside one of the hotels.

I waited.

Not for long in the first instance: Heinrich Schmidt
got out of the car, the tail car, and entered the basement
area of a house alongside the Volvo estate. When he
emerged, which was four minutes later, he had
Ogmanfiller with him. She was looking white and
scared, I thought; the news must have reached them by
now and they were getting out from under.

Brennan came out too, but no von Defflinger-
Zwickau. No Felicity.

Ogmanfiller and Schmidt got into the Volvo and were
joined by Louis X and the driver from the tail car.

The Volvo got moving immediately.

I followed, pulling out after a short interval. I didn't think I'd been spotted. Not yet, anyway. I could hardly expect anonymity to last for ever and it didn't. The Volvo took a right turn on two wheels and went along thereafter like a cat out of hell, dodging in and out of the traffic, causing chaos, and then continued at its headlong speed down a shopping precinct, scattering pedestrians, bouncing off a lamp standard and swinging hard right at the end. Also disregarding the law, I followed down the precinct. I saw then that I was coming into the dock area and a one-way system. The Volvo was going against the traffic flow; so did I. I did so until the Volvo braked very suddenly. As I veered right to pass it with the intention of swinging back in to block it, someone — Schmidt I think — opened fire. A bullet took my nearside front tyre and the car went out of control, though at that moment I was not moving fast. Not fast enough for any fatal effect, but I bumped my head hard on the pillar beside me and was dazed for long enough to allow Schmidt and Louis X to run back to get hold of me and drag me out with the Frenchman's knife nudging into my throat and drawing blood.

Being British none of the gawping motorists interfered. It just didn't pay to interfere: the police always stressed that. I was bundled into the Volvo, which at once drove on and came clear of the one-way system. I was down on the floorboards under Brennan's feet so I didn't see where we went, but it was a long way and I didn't believe we were remaining in the dock area.

Brennan was in a filthy mood, naturally. I was going to suffer. I'd ballsed the whole thing up obviously.

I didn't argue the point. They had me game, set and match. All I could think of to say was, 'You can't get away with it now, Brennan. You're in a corner and you know it.'

He knew it, all right. Not just the British police: his paymasters in Germany were not going to be pleased, and they might well have ways and means of dealing with him in a fairly fatal sense. So maybe he wouldn't be heading out for Germany after all.

I asked about Felicity, knowing what the answer would be.

Brennan said, 'She'll be going the same way as you, my friend.'

'Isn't it rather late,' I asked from the floorboards, 'for revenge?'

'Not for evidence,' he said, and he had a point I supposed. Felicity and myself apart, there was in fact nothing to link Brennan in with any of it. That was, just so long as he could get all his thugs away to safety with him. Leave any behind and they might crack.

When we stopped I had no idea where it was but it had to be somewhere along the coast for my money. I didn't see Brennan remaining in Britain any longer than he had to. And somewhere along the line we had to link up with Felicity: reasons as before − evidence. I felt a shiver run down my spine as I was hauled out of the Volvo in a garage, under electric light: there had always been more ways than one of disposing of evidence. And Brennan had never been short on ideas. Nevertheless, I had a feeling that Felicity was still alive. It would please Brennan to watch us both die together, and it would please him to watch my reaction when Felicity came under the final pressure.

The garage was an integral one with the outer door closed behind the Volvo's entry. Well guarded, I was taken through into the house. That house was in a state of near dilapidation and had an uninhabited feel about it, as though it had lingered for years behind a For Sale board. The door from the garage led into a passageway with bare, uncarpeted boards. From there I was taken into a room with one window, shuttered, no sight of daylight. My arms were held while I was once again roped, with extra bonds holding my wrists tight together.

I was pushed down to lie on the floor.

'No gag?' I asked sardonically.

Brennan laughed and said there was no need for gags: I could yell all I liked and no one would hear. 'There's no one around,' he said.

I asked where von Defflinger-Zwickau was. I said, 'I thought he had you by the short hairs, Brennan. Just in case you managed to knock off a bunch of German VIPs . . .'

'Which didn't happen.' Brennan swung away and left the room.

There was an eerie silence but over it and distantly I thought I heard sea sounds, the wash of water on a shore, the cries of seagulls. It was bitterly cold and there was a rising wind that I could hear battering at the walls of the house and shaking the window. There might be snow blowing along that wind. If so, then Brennan was likely to have a clear passage out to sea. I thought about those helicopters, snow-grounded already perhaps; I'd not heard them since I'd picked up the Volvo, though at that time there had been no snow.

I was left for a long time and I grew colder. Also hungry and thirsty. After a while I heard sounds from another room: the walls were thin, probably just hardboard partitions – they had that sort of look, hardboard papered over.

It was a radio. Brennan was listening to the BBC news broadcast. I gathered it was 6 p.m. I listened to the news reader's dispassionate tones: the G7 meeting was all set for the next day, the French Foreign Minister and the various heads of state were to attend a banquet that night at Buckingham Palace, the British Foreign Secretary had arrived in Paris and Le Shuttle had done its stuff in cementing the grand alliance of the European Community.

Absolutely no mention of the day's events in the control complex at Folkestone. Just one item that really gripped my attention: a man, believed to be a German national, had been found dead in the basement of a house in Folkestone. The body had been discovered by a neighbour whose dog had gone down the steps to the basement area and had disobeyed all calls to come up again, being glued to a prolonged sniffing at the outer door. The neighbour, identified as a Miss Crowshort, had discovered blood and had thereupon gone for the police.

And there was something else. A young woman had also been found when the police made their entry. Like the German, she had been shot. In her case the bullet had just missed the heart. She was undergoing surgery and would be questioned later. If she recovered.

I thought back a little way: I'd been wrong in thinking that Brennan would want to see us both die together. He hadn't, at that stage, wanted to tell me what had happened to Felicity. She had presumably to remain as some kind of hold over me.

Even if I died in the process, I was going to get Polecat Brennan.

Brennan came back in shortly after that broadcast.

I told him I'd heard it.

He made no response to that. All he said was, 'You'll be moving out in a few minutes.'

'Out to sea?'

'How did you guess?'

I asked another question. 'Where to, Brennan?'

He showed his teeth in a grin. 'Southern Ireland,' he said. 'Southern Ireland and safety.'

'From the Germans?'

'Never you mind,' Brennan said. 'In any case, you'll not be reaching Ireland yourself.'

That, I thought, could be taken as read. Finality loomed, somewhere out at sea.

But, although I didn't realize it at the time, Brennan had made a fatal error for himself.

16

It was full dark outside and there was a mantle of snow all around and more was coming down. But I was able to see where I was: Dungeness. No nearby dwellings, as Brennan had indicated earlier. The only lights were dim and distant, probably from the houses around the track of the miniature railway that ran from Hythe. I could just about make out the Dungeness light, distantly to the south. There was light too from what I took to be the airfield at Lydd, but I didn't suppose there would be any flying tonight. The sky was full of snow – very suitable for Brennan's trip to sea. That trip would most probably be similar to the trip from Germany: out in a small boat, to join a coaster at sea, a coaster that would put Brennan and his party ashore on some remote stretch of the Southern Irish shore, which was dotted with small bays and inlets and plenty of shielding rock.

'Right,' Brennan said.

I was given a shove from behind: Schmidt, using his gun as a prod. I went forward, stumbling over stones and small, grassy hillocks covered with snow. I heard the sea plainly now, a surge on shingle. There was a cold wind coming off the sea. Soon, through the gloom and the falling snow, I made out a boat lying off the shore. As we came nearer I saw the boat held just one man, keeping the boat in position by use of his oars. He evidently saw us approach; he pulled in closer, then lay off again in a couple of feet of water.

He called out something in an Irish accent, something I didn't catch. Behind me Schmidt said, 'Go right ahead. Get in the boat.'

We waded out. Brennan was in the lead, with Louis X beside him. They clambered aboard the boat, then reached down to drag me over the gunwale: trussed like a chicken ready for table, I was fairly unhandy.

Last to board was Ogmanfiller. When she was sitting on a thwart, we pulled out to sea, Brennan himself taking one of the oars. We went in total anonymity, in freezing cold with the snow falling like a Brennan-friendly blanket.

I wondered what was going on in Folkestone, in that hospital that Felicity had been taken to. The news broadcast hadn't gone into details about her, no indicating either way, likely recovery or possible death. I wondered what Max would be doing, what, if anything, he would learn from Felicity when she came round — if she came round. She might not have learned anything useful: Brennan wasn't the sort to give anything away. Not unless he'd said anything at the last, just before the shooting. Felicity appeared to me to be my last hope, and really it was a frail one. But at least she herself was free of Polecat Brennan whether she lived or died.

* * *

I'd been right about the coaster. It was a much more
sizable job than the vessel that had brought us from
Germany, at a guess I'd say about 1500 tons. Modern
construction: bridge and superstructure right aft, long
fo'c'sle with a deck cargo of containers. One man
leaned over the side as we made our approach, was
joined by another with whom he lowered a Jacob's
ladder over the side.

I said, 'Do you expect me to climb that?'

There was a consultation between Brennan and
Schmidt. It would be a case of hoisting me aboard by
use of a derrick — the vessel had a fairly high free-
board, too high for a man to reach down from deck
level.

Schmidt said, 'He can't do any harm now.'

Brennan agreed. Louis X was told to bring out his
knife, which he did.

'Careful,' I said, as the razor-sharp blade nicked a
wrist. I felt the run of blood. But it was a relief when the
ropes fell away. I was told to climb the ladder. As I
reached the bulwarks and dropped down to the deck,
Ogmanfiller came up. She was wearing trousers, so
there was no immodesty as she lifted a leg over the
bulwarks. After her, Brennan; then the others. The
small boat was cast adrift; no time for hoisting, any
more than there had been in my case. These men were in
a hurry. The moment we were all aboard, the engines
were put ahead and we turned to port, moving farther
out to sea before turning west again for Ireland.

I was shut in a spare cabin, with Heinrich Schmidt as guard.

I supposed they wanted to reach deeper water, somewhere in the middle of the Channel. From there, I wouldn't reappear all that soon. I assumed they meant to shoot me first.

After a while I put the question to Schmidt and he grinned. 'You have a personal interest?'

'You could say so.'

'Shooting,' he said. 'Alive would not be good. You could swim.'

'A long way to swim.'

'Persons have swum the Channel.'

'That's true,' I said. 'Anyway, don't let's dwell on it. Is there anything you want to tell me?'

'Before you die?'

'It's a way of putting it,' I said. 'But I just thought you might care to discuss the future. Your future. Such as, where do you and Brennan go from here? It seems to me you've rather lost out one way and another. Right?'

He said it wasn't right at all, they would make their comeback when Brennan was good and ready. Brennan, Schmidt said, had resources. Of course, I knew that. No doubt he had contacts with the IRA. I put this point. There was a superior smile on Schmidt's face but he didn't comment. But I kept the conversation going, simply because I felt the need to talk, to fill the gap between life and death, which was becoming a little fraught. I also had an idea that talking just might lead to Schmidt dropping his guard, giving me a chance to make a grab for his gun.

But that didn't happen. Schmidt was right on the ball all the way through.

Our little chat was interrupted by the internal-communication telephone on the bulkhead. Schmidt, keeping his gun carefully on me, answered. He listened. He hung the phone back on its hook. He gestured with his gun. 'It is now,' he said. 'Go ahead of me to the deck.'

I had taken my chance and I'd taken it good. Schmidt went up that ladder just a little too close behind. As I reached the top, I lashed out with a foot and caught him smack in his upturned face. There was an oath and a crash and I dropped back down the ladder and landed on Schmidt. I grabbed for his gun, got it in my hands, and smashed the butt into his face and then put him right out of action by a smashing blow to his head.

Then I saw Louis X looking down. I fired point blank and he seemed to vanish totally. There were no more faces but of course they would be waiting.

I went up the ladder, taking it fast rather than carefully, not wanting to give Brennan or the vessel's crew time to regroup as it were. I came over the top of the hatch firing in a wide arc and saw two men go down. I didn't know who they were — crew probably. I didn't see Brennan. But I did hear Ogmanfiller screeching from somewhere above, the bridge probably. What she yelled out in a panic was interesting; and a moment later

I heard for myself what she was on about: the unmistakable sound of a helicopter. The sky had cleared now, though it was still night, and seconds later I saw the copter moving in, tilted down towards us, losing height.

From behind me, from a canvas-covered cargo hatch abaft the containers of the deck cargo, someone fired. A bullet scraped my cheek, and I was round in a flash, firing back with another wide spread. I saw a man go down and I believe it was Brennan; there was no time to make certain. A moment later more firing came from the bridge, gunfire directed at the helicopter.

The helicopter's crew replied to that fire. I saw a number of flashes of what I believe was cannonfire loosed on the deck of the coaster. I was aware of large holes appearing in a long line across the canvas cover of the hatch, and a splintering of woodwork was revealed in the beam of a searchlight from the helicopter. The cannon shells had penetrated the wooden hatch-planks.

That, apart from a gigantic sheet of flame and a deafening roar was the last thing I remembered.

I came to in hospital. As it turned out, the same hospital as Felicity had been taken to. I came round remarkably clear-headed. The first thing they told me was that Felicity was doing well and should be out of hospital in a week or so. They told me I'd been yanked from the sea by the helicopter's winchman, more or less undamaged, just a broken leg and arm and temporary concussion.

The coaster had vanished, they said. Nothing left but

floating debris, all hands blown to pieces. And that would include Polecat Brennan. And Schmidt and Louis X. And Ogmanfiller. A clean sweep, what with Gerhardt von Defflinger-Zwickau dead already in that Folkestone basement.

Later, Max came down to see me. With Hedge, Hedge being beside himself with a mixture of joy and foreboding. The coaster, he said, had evidently been carrying contraband: explosives, which explained a lot.

'For the IRA?' I asked.

'Most probably, in our opinion. We must be very careful — there is no proof.' Hedge was speaking a little above a whisper, looking around himself cautiously as though a spy might lie concealed beneath my bed. 'I fear there may be trouble with Dublin. It's all very unfortunate, that part of it. Such a pity.'

I stared at him. 'Pity my backside.' I saw him bridle at that. 'The threat was aborted — *I* can't claim any kudos for that. But what we set out to do has been done. Hasn't it?'

Hedge conceded the point. 'Oh, yes, yes indeed it has. But it was such a pity it had to be ended finally by gunfire.'

I managed to suppress the rude, one-word answer that he deserved. I said, 'I suppose you'd have settled it by diplomacy,' and he nodded his head vigorously, stupid sod. It was Max who came across with the really interesting information.

He said, 'If you're wondering how that helicopter picked you up — '

'Sheer luck,' I said.

He shook his head. 'Not so. A series of signals was intercepted. Your voice, as a matter of fact. You homed the helicopter onto the ship — there were some earlier interceptions that pointed up the Dungeness area. Can you explain how that happened, Shaw?'

I blew out a long breath of amazement. Brennan had really done himself in. I told Max about that little bug I'd been made to swallow and which would now mean an operation for its removal from my gut. Perhaps it had been Schmidt's own bright idea, not Brennan's. We would never know now.